Abigay's Farm

Odette Elliott

To Zahrya
from
David and
Marjorie

SilverWood

Best wishes
Odette

Published in 2021 by SilverWood Books

SilverWood Books Ltd
14 Small Street, Bristol, BS1 1DE, United Kingdom
www.silverwoodbooks.co.uk

ISBN 978-1-80042-133-2 (paperback)
ISBN 978-1-80042-188-2 (ebook)

British Library Cataloguing in Publication Data
A CIP catalogue record for this book is
available from the British Library

Page design and typesetting by SilverWood Books

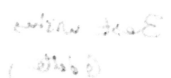

To granddaughters Kaymen and Zakeya with love

To be a farmer and have the privilege of working the land, caring for animals and living hand in hand with nature is a wonderful thing. However, it is not always plain sailing as the financial returns for hours and hours of hard work can almost be non-existent, and sometimes, in order to save their beloved farm as well as their way of life, farmers must 'take the bull by the horns' and diversify.

This beautifully written book shows how the bond of a farming family to one another (and to their farm) is so strong that it gives them the grit and courage to overcome obstacles and secure a bright future for Willowfield Farm."

Janet Legge, Shortwood Farm

Chapter 1

WILLOWFIELD

They're up to something, I thought, as I looked at the man and boy walking towards us along the bumpy lane.

Even at that distance, I knew who they were – Christopher King and his dad.

We slowed down by the prickly hawthorn bush to let them pass. Christopher turned slowly and fixed me with an evil grin. It made my stomach churn.

Mum stopped the car at the entrance to the farm.

Usually there's a race between me and my twin Gabriel to get to the big gate first. This time, I couldn't move. This time, there was no Gabriel beside me.

'It's OK, Abigay,' said Mum, unbuckling her seat belt and getting out. 'I'll do it.'

The bolt clattered as she slid it sideways and the gate swung open slowly with a loud squeak. The farm cats jumped off the log pile and disappeared in a flash of black and white and ginger.

As we drove into the farmyard, I looked at the old house with the climbing rose reaching right up to the bedroom windows. Soon it would be in full bloom, covered in yellow roses. Willowfield has always been a special place full of memories for Gabriel and me.

We're always begging Mum or Dad to bring us to the farm from London. And when we're not there, we think about it – a lot!

Last year when the Big Blizzard hit, we were so worried. We saw a photo of the snow reaching to the top of the hedges and we had visions of our grandparents digging their way to the milking parlour and cowshed, and struggling to feed the hens and all the animals.

It was early spring now and I could hear the lambs bleating way off in the fields.

Grandma was waiting. As soon as she saw us, her face lit up. She wiped her hands on her apron and brushed back her silvery grey hair, before wrapping me all alone in a big hug. It felt strange. Usually, she puts an arm round both me and Gabriel – one on each side and gives us each a big squeeze.

'I love the way you've brushed your curls. Now I can actually see your face!' she said with a laugh. 'And you've grown again. You're taller than me now.'

Mum was taking the bags out of the car when Grandpa arrived on his sit-on mower, white hair blowing all over the place, as usual.

'Just getting the garden shipshape,' he called out.

Something in his voice told me he wasn't his usual self – probably because of Gabriel. Or was it to do with Mr King and Christopher? What were they doing walking away from the farm just now? They must have been visiting. Why?

Inside the farmhouse kitchen, everything looked the same – the gleaming copper kettle and Grandma's collection of blue and white plates and funny teapots. So much had changed for us these last few months but Willowfield is the one thing that never changes.

'Come and look at the garden,' said Grandpa, before I could follow Mum and Grandma into the conservatory. 'You don't want to be sitting down after such a long drive, do you? Come and see our flowers. We've still got a few daffodils and tulips in bloom. We're a bit behind you London folks.'

The flowers were bright and cheerful – a mass of yellow and red. I wanted to be cheerful too but today it just wasn't possible.

We walked to the pond and stopped.

Gabriel and I always used to spend ages there looking for tadpoles and frogs in the spring and getting covered head to toe in mud. In summer, we watched the dragonflies hover and dart above the surface of the water. They looked so ancient. 'Dragonflies evolved 300 million years ago,' Gabriel would say.

A small wind ruffled the surface of the water and made me shiver.

'It's a bit cold today,' Grandpa said. 'Let's go and have a peep at Rosie instead.'

Rosie the donkey recognised me straight away. I stroked her shaggy mane and rough grey coat and she nuzzled up against me.

'Sorry, Rosie,' I whispered in her ear. 'Gabriel's not here.'

Suddenly, the wind swirled up again and whipped the dust round the farmyard.

'We'd better go in now,' said Grandpa. 'I don't know how long your Mum has before driving back to London.'

Mum gave me a new notebook just before she left.

'You can use it to write down your feelings if you like,' she said. 'Or for your drawings. And don't worry, I know you miss Gabriel, love, but it will all be alright. Anyway, we'll speak tomorrow,' she called through the open window as she drove off.

We waited by the gate until the car became a tiny speck where the lane joins the main road. Then we walked back slowly to the house.

All evening Grandma was extra jolly. I felt she was only doing it for my benefit. As for Grandpa, he wasn't listening to a word Grandma and I were saying.

At bedtime, Grandma came up with me.

'No, not that one this time,' she said, as I made my way into the room Gabriel and I share with the bunk beds and all our favourite books.

'I'm putting you into the small room looking onto the farm garden and the pond.'

'Why not the usual one?' I asked.

'Grandpa still hasn't mended the loose barn roof,' Grandma said with a sigh. 'It's so noisy when the wind blows. It will only keep you awake.'

When Grandma left the room, I sat for a minute. Then, I reached for my phone and wrote:

Guess what? I'm in a different bedroom???
And Grandma and Grandpa are being extra weird!!!

I'll send another message tomorrow

Ping! …Message sent to Gabriel.

Chapter 2

AUNTIE RACHEL

They say things don't look so bad after a good night's sleep. And it's true.

The sun poured through the gap in the curtains and shone straight on my face. I blinked and remembered where I was.

I could hear Grandma moving around downstairs in the kitchen.

I slipped out of bed and pulled on a pair of faded dungarees. The cool morning air made me shiver as I tiptoed downstairs. The stone floor felt cold under my bare feet as I crossed the kitchen.

Grandma was leaning over the range, stirring a large pan of porridge. I crept up behind her and wrapped my arms around her. She turned and smiled.

'It's so lovely to have you back, Abigay!' she said squeezing me tight. 'I still can't believe how much you've grown. You'll be lifting me up soon,' she laughed.

'Here you go,' she said suddenly, handing me the wicker

basket. 'Time to do your job.'

I took the basket and made my way to the back door. Grabbing a fleece from the porch, I stepped into a pair of wellies and set off across the yard.

Standing on an upturned bucket in front of the door to the chicken shed, I peered in at the hens inside, all safe from any foxes.

'Hello my beauties!' I said.

When I opened the door, they hurried out gleefully, pecking and clucking. I put my hands in the nesting boxes and found six eggs, all warm to touch. I put each one carefully in the basket before making my way back across the yard.

'Six this morning!' I shouted, coming into the kitchen.

Grandma put the heavy frying pan on the range. I cracked the eggs and slid them into the pan. We added the rashers of bacon which were soon sizzling loudly. The kitchen filled with the most delicious smell – the smell of the first morning back at the farm.

Grandma looked at the clock. 'I wonder where your grandfather is? He should have finished milking by now.'

As if by magic, Grandpa suddenly appeared in the kitchen.

'I'm starving,' he announced. 'Where's that breakfast we were all promised?'

At the farm we don't talk much during meals because the food is always soooo good! All you can hear is the sound of clinking, clattering, munching, and crunching, with the odd 'ahh' or 'mmm' thrown in.

'Come with me, Abigay,' said Grandpa, when he had finished slurping down the last of his tea. 'I've got something to show you.'

I followed him outside and he led me round to the side of the house. A new swing hung from a branch of the apple tree.

Honestly, I thought when I saw it. How old does Grandpa think I am? Doesn't he remember we're in our first year at the secondary school? But when I sat on the swing and looked up at the ropes tied high in the branches, I felt like I was floating on air.

'It's perfect!' I said. 'Thank you.' And I meant it. 'This will be a great thinking place!' After a minute, I looked up at Grandpa.

'Gabriel's back in hospital,' I said in a quiet voice. 'His hip is painful again and he can hardly walk.'

Grandpa nodded thoughtfully.

'I know it's hard, Abigay, but you have to trust the doctors. They'll take good care of him.'

'I suppose so,' I said.

Grandpa gave me a half-smile. He seemed to become distracted then. He turned and wandered off without a word. That was odd.

I stayed on the swing for a long time – sometimes soaring up high, sometimes just sitting still. I tried to call Gabriel but he didn't answer. I swung slowly. Then I shut my eyes. The sun felt warm on my face as blurry light patterns filtered through my eyelids.

'Where's my favourite niece?' a familiar voice rang out.

It was Auntie Rachel. I'm her *only* niece but she always says that.

I jumped off the swing and ran to meet her. She appeared holding a mug of coffee.

Auntie Rachel is always fun to be with almost like an older sister. She's actually Mum's younger sister although she doesn't look like Mum at all. She's got long flowing brown hair and lives in jeans and T-shirts when she's not working. And because she's a teacher, she has school holidays just like us. Her school is in the city, not where she lives in the village.

'I like your hairstyle!' Auntie said.

'I've got a new spray!' I replied. 'From the Afro hair care shop on our high street.'

'It looks great. So, let's go and see Beauty then,' she said.

'Of course!' I said.

Beauty is Auntie Rachel's Welsh pony. She keeps her at the farm. 'Just as well,' Grandma often says. 'Otherwise, I'd never get to see my younger daughter either.'

We wandered up the slope towards the field.

'How does Gabriel feel about being back in hospital?' Auntie Rachel asked, suddenly serious.

'I'm not sure,' I said. 'He's got help with the pain. I think he's OK.'

Auntie Rachel nodded. 'He's a brave lad. You both need to hang in there,' she added.

Beauty is an amazing chestnut-brown with a white tail, four white "socks" and the sweetest nature ever.

'Her coat looks so shiny,' I said.

Auntie Rachel smiled. 'Yes, she looks well. She's pregnant, you know.'

She laughed when she saw my face.

'The vet came a couple of days ago. She's keeping an eye on her as this is her first foal but she's pleased with her condition. It's a good time of the year for a foal to be born, before the heat of the summer.'

Auntie Rachel bought Beauty from her friend Greta when she and her family moved to the United States for work two years ago. She was so excited to bring her back to Willowfield.

We gave her some high quality hay and grain – nothing but the best for our Beauty. We patted her and stroked her nose – that's the thing about her, she loves all the attention.

We talked about books…then Gabriel again…and school. Auntie Rachel is always interested in what we're up to.

Later, sitting in the bay window, I sent another message to Gabriel.

ME:

Hey! How are you feeling?
Are you missing me?
I've been round the farm, even down to the stream
where we had that argument with Christopher King
last year when he said all those horrible things about
Willowfield.
Rosie says hee-haw to you btw.
Grandma has some new chickens that look like they have
feathery bed socks!
And there's a lot of new piglets.
Also Auntie Rachel was here – she says you're brave.

The reply came immediately.

GABRIEL:

I'm OK sort of.
All sounds good at the farm.
Yeah, let's hope Christopher King stays away.

I quickly changed the subject.

ME:

Oh, by the way, I forgot to say something really important.
What do you get when you cross a robot and a tractor?
.... Give up???
A transfarmer!!!

GABRIEL:
Ha, ha, very funny...or should I say, GROAN!

They say you should never tempt fate. And maybe that's what I did when I mentioned Christopher. Little did I know that I would be seeing him soon enough – actually, very soon! And it would change everything!

Chapter 3

CHRISTOPHER

'**Another local farmer sells up**' screamed the headline in the Herefordshire Gazette.

'Sorry, Abigay, just need to check the horoscope,' said Grandma sliding the paper away as I started to read. 'Don't you worry about farming problems,' she added.

Grandma and Grandpa are getting odder by the day, I thought to myself. Sometimes, I would catch them talking quietly so I couldn't hear. Or the conversation would suddenly *stop* when I entered the room.

And don't even start me on 'the paperwork'. They were constantly doing 'paperwork' and working on 'figures'. Normally, they were both busy with the animals and we would follow them around everywhere like ducklings. I'd never heard of them working on 'paperwork' or 'figures' before!

And it all became even stranger. I was feeding the hens when Grandpa wandered past.

'By the way, Fred King is passing by this afternoon,' he

said. 'We have some business to discuss.'

Fred King is Christopher's dad. He never comes to discuss business. He never comes, full stop. And that wasn't the worst of it.

'He'll be bringing Christopher,' added Grandpa.

He must have seen the look of horror on my face.

'"Christopher can be company for Abigay, since Gabriel isn't here", is what Mr King said.'

Company for Abigay! I thought. Honestly, I need Christopher's company like I need a hole in the head – as Grandma would say.

'Just because Gabriel's not here doesn't mean I have to hang around with Christopher King,' I said to Grandpa.

'Well, what's done is done,' he said quietly.

Fred King and Christopher arrived soon after lunch. Christopher got out of the car and lumbered after his dad, looking all around the yard. He was a miniature version of his dad, all red-faced and spotty.

He's always busy trying to act superior but even though he's taller, he's only about six months older than us.

Gabriel and I reckon he's got the mean gene – he just can't help himself. Every time he opens his mouth, something nasty comes out.

Grandma listed off the farm rules to both of us in the kitchen. This is sooooo embarrassing! I thought. The last time Grandma explained the rules, I must have been about six.

DON'T throw anything in the pond
DON'T touch the farm machinery
DON'T go into the field with the cows and calves
If you open a gate, shut it behind you.

Christopher replied with a short 'Yep' for each rule, all the while looking around and trying to appear as bored as possible.

He knows farm rules too, living on the farm next to ours – worst luck – but I realised Grandma didn't trust him, especially if it's someone else's farm.

As soon as Grandma had finished, he rushed out.

I caught up with him by the pond.

Splash! A large rock landed in the murky water.

'Don't do that!' I shouted.

He turned to me.

'Has your brother still got that leg brace thing?'

'No,' I said.

'So, what's wrong with him anyway?'

'You wouldn't understand,' I said, 'and besides, it's none of your business.'

'Fair enough!' he said and lobbed another rock into the pond. It made a deep "plunk" as it broke the surface, followed by a huge splash.

'Your pond's boring!' he said and rushed off again.

Now where's he going, I thought. We were supposed to stay together – that's what Grandma said – and I was beginning to understand why.

I found him beyond the silage pit next to the bull pen.

He was kicking the metal fence, annoying the Hereford bull. Eventually he stopped and fixed me with his beady eyes.

'You know what,' he said, 'your grandparents are too old to be running a farm. Me and my dad are going to buy this place. And then it's bye, bye Willowfield for you.'

He went silent then and looked over at the farm door,

watching for when his dad would come out.

I couldn't believe what I just heard. I wanted to open the metal gate and let the Hereford bull charge straight at him. Instead, I froze. I couldn't speak. At that moment, what I needed most was to talk to Grandma and Grandpa – *urgently*!

After the Kings had gone, I went into the kitchen.

'Are you selling the farm?' I demanded.

Grandpa didn't answer. He switched the kettle on, sat down on his chair and stared ahead. Grandma didn't say anything either. She was suddenly very busy cleaning the sink.

'Well, Christopher King seems to think so. How come I don't know anything about this?'

Grandpa gave a deep sigh.

'Who knows what the future holds,' he said. 'All the small farmers round here are trying to make more money to survive. But things will get better soon – you'll see.'

Suddenly, Grandma pushed her chair backwards. It made a sharp, scraping noise on the tiles. She went to the back door.

'Abigay, I'm going for a walk. Come with me.'

A walk was just what I needed. And besides, if Grandpa wasn't telling me anything, maybe Grandma would!

Chapter 4

THE THREE MACS

Grandma hurried across the farmyard. She stopped and waited for me by the old barn. When I caught up with her, she pointed to the roof.

'Look! That's why you're not in your usual room.'

I could see part of the corrugated iron roof hanging down loosely.

'That needs fixing. When the wind blows, it makes an awful rattle – day and night. Before, your grandfather would be up there in a shot to fix it. Now, he just doesn't care!'

She sighed deeply. 'Your grandpa says he's not worried, things will get better. But at this rate they won't!

'We've suggested lots of ideas to make money – pick your own fruit, solar panels, wind turbines…plenty of others too – but Grandpa has said no to *everything*!

'I don't know what's got into him. Why is he not even *trying?*'

I wasn't exactly sure whether Grandma was talking to

me or the five cows still in the shed, but when she paused, they all mooed suddenly.

Grandma blinked and then suddenly relaxed.

'I'm sorry, Abigay. You shouldn't have to hear all that. You have enough to worry about with Gabriel. Tell you what, let's do a proper walk!'

We headed out past the bank of primroses towards the wood on the ridge.

Grandma always makes us look at the flowers as well as the crops and animals. She teaches us all the names and then tests us. Since last time, I had studied all the spring flowers, so I felt sure Grandma would be impressed.

Primroses and violets were easy. Grandma told me there's a flower a bit like a primrose called a cowslip. The proper name is Primula veris but I much prefer cowslip – it still makes me laugh.

Just before entering the wood, Grandma pointed to some bright little white flowers. 'Lesser stitchwort,' she announced, then laughed at my expression.

'I thought they were called Billy's buttons,' I said. 'I like that name way more than wort.'

The next one was a windflower. It was white but ever so slightly pink as well. It looked delicate – just like its name.

As we looked down the slope from the path, Grandma pointed out the badger setts in the clearing. We stopped and checked out the mound and the many exit and entry tunnels.

'These badgers have been here for generations!' Grandma said. 'One day, when Gabriel is better, we'll come into the wood at night. If we're lucky, we might see them digging around for food or even spy the young ones playing!'

'Gabriel will definitely be up for that!' I said.

As we came out of the top wood, a mauve and white campervan pulled up at the head of the drive and a man leaned out of the window.

'Say, lady,' he asked in a loud voice, 'can you tell me if the farmer's in?' He sounded American.

Grandma looked at him crossly.

'You can talk to me,' she said. 'My husband Edward Woolgar and I own this farm.'

'Oh. Sorry, ma'am! I'm just wondering if we can camp in one of your fields for a few days. We've got everything we need and won't be any bother. And we're happy to pay your usual fee.'

Grandma thought for a bit. 'OK,' she said. 'You can camp in this top field. Fresh water is available from the tap by the milking parlour opposite the farmhouse. You just go down the drive that way,' she pointed. 'Oh! And remember, if you open a gate, to shut it behind you. We'll come and see you later to see how you're getting along.'

The man gave a thumbs up and drove the van slowly into the top field. I could see a young girl looking out of the window. She grinned and waved.

We followed them over to where they had parked. They seemed friendly – a man and a woman. The girl had disappeared.

'We're the Three Macs,' said the man, jumping down from the driving seat.

He had grey hair tied back in a ponytail and he flashed a beaming smile every time he spoke.

'Our proper name is Mackenzie. I'm Dave, by the way,' he added, firmly shaking hands with Grandma and then with me.

'And I'm Tammy,' said the woman who suddenly appeared beside him.

She had bright auburn hair tied back with a lime-green scarf. They were wearing such weird, colourful clothes, that I wasn't surprised by what she said next.

'We're artists. I paint and Dave does woodcarvings. We just love your beautiful countryside. Like that wood over there, or those small fields with the rolling hills beyond. In Canada, it's all so different.'

Tammy could see that I was looking at the blur of red shorts running round the field in the distance.

'As you can see, our Juliette doesn't like sitting still,' she laughed. 'She needs to let off steam as we've been travelling all afternoon. I guess she'll come and make friends with you soon enough.'

When it was time for me and Grandma to get back and feed the hens, we headed down the field. As we walked, we chatted about the strange French-Canadian family.

'Are they all like that in Canada, I wonder?' said Grandma.

Later I sent a text to Gabriel.

ME:

Hey whatcha doin? – bet you thought I'd forgotten you!

GABRIEL:

Not much. Where have you been?
What's happening?

24

ME:

Well, latest farm news from Willowfield:
the bantam hen has had six chicks, all different colours –
grey, white, speckled, yellow, brown, black!

GABRIEL:

Who tells the best chicken jokes?
Apart from me? Give up?
Comedihens!!!

ME:

Groan! No, triple groan!
So, more news: a crazy but nice French-Canadian family
are camping with their campervan in the top field.

GABRIEL:

Oh, tell me more…
actually, don't, they're bringing the food!
Gotta go. Speak tomorrow.

I deliberately didn't tell Gabriel about Christopher King and his dad – or Grandma's outburst. Instead, I reached for Mum's notebook and drew a picture of Christopher falling head first into the pond. I drew my hand pushing him with my arm disappearing off the edge of the page. His eyes looked all googly and frightened with his hair sticking out in all directions. I added a speech bubble near the edge of the page and wrote:

This farm is not for sale!!!

Chapter 5

JULIETTE

The garden gate squeaked softly; then someone tapped loudly on the door. Usually, people just knock, open the door and walk straight in.

'Come in!' Grandma called out but nothing happened. She got up and opened the door.

A girl with fair hair tied in two bunches was jumping up and down excitedly on the doorstep. It was Juliette, the Three Macs girl. Up close, she looked way younger than me – maybe about eight years old.

'My mum said not to bother you, so I just came to say hi!'

Grandma laughed. 'You better come in then. We didn't get to say hello properly yesterday, did we?'

'Hi!' I said.

Juliette gazed wide-eyed round the kitchen, then looked straight at me.

'Tammy told me you're a twin,' she said. 'Where's your brother? I've never seen boy and girl twins.'

It was difficult to explain about Gabriel without talking about his illness but Juliette seemed interested. I told her about him being in hospital and she listened without interrupting.

'That's bad luck,' she said.

Nobody spoke for a moment.

'Why don't I show you round the farm?' I said.

'Yes, pleeease!' said Juliette, clapping her hands.

'Grandma, can we go and see if there are any eggs?' I asked.

'Of course!' said Grandma, giving me the basket. 'Show Juliette what to do – and don't forget to tell her the farm ru...'

'Rules!' Juliette interrupted. 'I know about the rules – Tammy, my mother told me all about shutting the gates and everything. I'll be careful, I promise!'

I took Juliette to the hen house where we found six white eggs and three lovely brown ones. She handled them more carefully and gently than I expected.

'They're still warm,' she said, surprised.

After we took the eggs back, we headed out again.

We heard the sound of wings beating against the air. We looked up and caught sight of two ducks flying low over our heads. They were coming in fast but managed to do a perfect landing right in the middle of the pond – what Gabriel calls their 'Emergency Stop'!

The drake ruffled its beautiful dark blue and green feathers.

'I want to see the WHOLE FARM!' Juliette said. Standing still didn't seem to suit her at all. She set off like a puppy in a hurry.

'Wait a minute!' I said as she scrambled over the first gate.

'One day, I'm going to be a famous gymnast,' she shouted. 'I have to practise whenever I can. Do you know why I'm in such a hurry? Because I'm sooooo excited! I've never been to a farm like this before. In Canada, farms are *huge* and the fields go on *forever*.'

'What about city farms?' I said. 'In London we went to the city farm all the time with our primary school.'

'I don't go to school,' said Juliette.

'What? Isn't it against the law not to go to school?'

'I'm home-schooled – Tammy and Dave are my teachers.'

I thought it was strange that she called her parents by their first names. It was even stranger that they were her *teachers*! Juliette prattled on about home-schooling but I wasn't really listening.

She wanted to see the whole farm, so I decided to take her down to the stream at the bottom of the hill.

To get to there, we had to walk through stinging nettles. Without wellies to protect us, it was hard. When we finally got there, our legs were covered in red marks.

'Don't scratch them,' I told Juliette. 'It'll just make it worse.'

The stream was more like a trickle.

'This isn't much fun,' Juliette said, sounding disappointed.

'Usually, there's way more water,' I said.

Gabriel and I love it down there. It's one of our favourite places. But Juliette was soon bored. I was really starting to miss Gabriel. He wouldn't have been bored.

Juliette didn't want to stay, so we hurried back up the hill.

'Let's play hide-and-seek round the farmyard,' she said.

'You mustn't touch the farm machines,' I said. 'It's another rule. And don't fall into the pond or tease the bull.'

Juliette thought for a minute. 'Let's have a race instead, up to that shed and back.'

'Alright,' I said doubtfully. Even as I said it, I knew it was a *bad* idea.

Juliette dashed off to the pond, ran all around the far edge, and headed straight for the cowshed.

'Not the cowshed!' I yelled panting behind her, as she raced into the yard with the cow muck oozing out, all brown and slippery.

'STOP!' I shouted again, but it was too late. Juliette slid about two metres. Her legs slipped from under her and she fell hard on her bum. I rushed to help and did exactly the same. We were both smeared and splattered in brown, slimy cow poo!

Yeuuuuuuuuuch!

As for the smell, don't even ask. It was like the stench of rotten eggs times ten!

Oh no! I thought, as I struggled to get up. There's going to be TROUBLE!

Chapter 6

CAMPERVAN

I staggered back to the house and Juliette limped back to her mum. I wasn't looking forward to Grandma's reaction. Why didn't I stop Juliette running in the farmyard? I thought.

She stood with her hands on her hips and sighed a long, loud sigh when she saw the mess I was in and smelt the dreadful stink I had brought into the house.

'Well, I don't suppose you could have stopped her,' she said shaking her head.

That's when we heard Grandpa arrive. He kicked his boots off in the porch and came into the kitchen – with Juliette! She was holding a bath towel. Grandpa looked confused.

'I met this young'un in the farmyard,' he said. 'She said her mother asked if she could have a shower in our house as she's too messy to clean up in the *van*? Does anyone know who she is or what she's talking about?'

Juliette just stood there grinning and saying 'Stinkypoo!'

There was a flicker of a smile on Grandma's face.

'I'll explain later,' she said to Grandpa. 'You'd better come in, Juliette,' she said. 'As soon as Abigay has had a shower, you can have one too.'

We felt much better afterwards sitting in our bathrobes in the conservatory.

That's when Tammy arrived. 'I'm so, so sorry Mr and Mrs Woolgar,' she said. 'And thank you so much for letting Juliette use the shower.'

She turned to me. 'Why don't you get dressed and come and see our campervan? I'll make waffles and then I'll give you both some art paper, pencils and paints. I hope you like drawing, Abigay.'

'I do,' I said. 'And I'd love to come!'

The van didn't look very big on the outside, but just like Doctor Who's Tardis, it was really big inside. There were cupboards for everything. Juliette opened them all.

'Ta-Dah! My clothes,' she said. 'Ta-Dah! Tammy's and Dave's clothes. A cupboard for plates, one for saucepans. Ta-Dah! One for my knickers and T-shirts.' She giggled.

I was impressed. Everything was neatly folded.

She pointed to two gas rings. 'That's the cooker. Guess where the sink is.' She looked all around with fake wide eyes, then she lifted up a wooden tray. 'Ta-Dah! It's under here!'

'Where are the beds?' I asked. 'Where do you sleep?'

'We fix the table differently and move all the cushions on top to make a double bed. My bed's a hammock hanging from the roof,' she laughed. 'We hook it up every evening.'

'It's like a jigsaw puzzle,' I said. 'It's AMAZING!'

We ate waffles with Canadian maple syrup until we nearly burst. Then Tammy cleared the table and put on an artist's smock with smudges of paint all over it.

'I'm off for a bit now. The light is good today and I want to paint the view looking down on the farmyard.'

She gave us each three big sheets of paper and some smaller, thinner sheets. 'This art paper is quite special,' said Tammy. 'So have a little think before you start drawing, or practise on the lighter paper first. Dave is working outside and he'll pop in to see how you're getting on.'

When Tammy Mac had gone, Juliette giggled. 'I'm going to draw a picture of me slipping in the poo!'

'I'm going to think first,' I said.

Maybe I was still wondering about how the farm might make money, but I suddenly had a picture in my head of the top field full of tents and campervans and children playing and mums and dads relaxing and cooking on camping stoves.

Juliette put her pencil down and looked at me. 'What is it?'

I don't know why I started to talk to Juliette then – she's way too young – but Gabriel wasn't there and he had his own problems anyway, Grandma and Grandpa wouldn't discuss *anything* with me, and Mum, Dad and Auntie Rachel were far too busy to talk.

'Grandma told me that lots of small farms are looking for ways to survive,' I said. 'Some farmers are even selling up – I couldn't bear it if Willowfield got sold.'

Juliette was silent for once so I just kept going.

'My mum and dad never wanted to be farmers, you know. They love their jobs in London too much – they're doing medical research. But Gabriel and I just love this place. It's so special. It's our family farm and we want it to stay that way. Right now, Gabriel is very sick and in pain, and the idea of us losing the farm is the last thing he needs to hear.'

'So, what's your idea?' Juliette asked with a puzzled look.

'Well, why not turn the top field into a proper campsite? Campers pay to camp, so it would bring in extra money. But I need to make Grandpa think that a campsite is a brilliant idea! So… I'll draw a picture of a really busy campsite and put pound signs and coins and twenty-pound notes all around the edge. Then, I casually leave it on the kitchen table, Grandpa sees it, the idea is planted in his head. He then thinks it's *his* idea! Then he sets up a campsite for real, we make loads of money and the farm is saved – ta-dah!'

I was starting to sound like Juliette. I know I was being silly but I had to dream.

First, I drew the outline of the Three Macs' campervan near the bottom of the page. Then I added lots of tents and campervans – expanding upwards and outwards. The camp grew and grew until it started to look like one of those giant Where's Wally illustrations that we used to look at when we were little. Juliette had her arm over her picture to stop me looking at it. She had her tongue out the way really small kids do. You had to laugh. We didn't even notice when Dave wandered in.

'Oh! My goodness! What concentration!' he said, looking at the pictures.

'There seems to be a common theme here. Campervans and tents – interesting.'

'We're going to get Abigay's grandpa to start a proper campsite,' said Juliette. 'And these are the posters to make him think it's a good idea. Abigay says it's because the farm's losing money and we mustn't say anything to her twin Gabriel because he's in hospital with a nasty disease called Perthes in his hip and he'll be upset.'

'I'm very sorry to hear that,' said Dave when Juliette had recovered her breath. 'I do hope he gets well soon.' He was silent for a moment.

'Isn't this field a bit small for a campsite?' he suddenly said.

'Well, we've got to do something or we won't have a field for much longer,' I said.

Dave looked puzzled.

'And why so urgent?' he asked, looking really concerned.

I wasn't used to grown-ups taking an interest like this – it felt different.

'It's like Juliette said, the farm's losing money. And Mr King, the neighbouring farmer, is trying to swipe it from under us. But we won't let him – Willowfield is our farm.'

I felt tears prickling my eyes but I was determined not to cry, not in front of Dave and *especially* not in front of Juliette.

Chapter 7

IDEAS

Dave had a way of speaking slowly and quietly. It made you listen to him.

'I get that you're worried, Abigay,' he said. 'But there's two bits of advice I can give you. Come up with lots of ideas and think *big*!'

'But even if kids do think really BIG, who's going to listen?' I said. 'Grown-ups don't listen most of the time anyway.'

'Well, if the idea is imaginative and exciting enough, people *will* listen. If it's really big, then it will also need money to get it going.

'Your grandparents could get a loan from the bank and pay it back when they start to earn some money.' He laughed. 'Well, that's the end of today's lecture, by Dr Dave of Montreal!'

'So, what do I do about this then?' I said, holding up my poster.

'Well, apart from it being an *excellent* piece of artwork

– you should show Tammy, by the way – it's also Idea Number One, your starting point.

'You need to come up with a whole heap of other ideas. Write down as many as you can, no matter how stupid they may seem, then choose the best ones.

'So, I'm off now to work on my bird sculpture. I've just started it. Later, I'll let you guess what bird you think it's going to be.'

'OK,' I said when Dave had gone. 'Let's do a list then.'

Juliette banged her forehead with the heel of her hand.

'It helps me to come up with all my fantastic wizardly ideas!' she said when she saw me looking puzzled.

Juliette is not at all bothered about boasting, I thought. She certainly wouldn't get away with it at our school. But now there was no time to lose. We needed to get some good ideas down!

'But I don't know anything about farms in the UK,' said Juliette. 'All I know is in Canada it would take two whole days to drive a tractor across a single field of wheat.'

'Grandpa had a tractor like that once,' I laughed. 'He had to get rid of it in the end and buy a better one.'

The joke was wasted on Juliette. She looked confused. Gabriel would've got it, I thought.

'Well, OK,' I said. 'But don't give up. I bet you've got loads of ideas.'

In among the crazy ones, I thought.

'You can sell things at the gate,' Juliette said suddenly. 'We saw signs with "Fresh Eggs for Sale" and "Jam for Sale" on the way here.'

'That's actually good,' I said. 'Let's start with that.'

1. Jam and eggs for sale

My pencil was poised to write down more and it stayed like that for a long while. Then suddenly, an idea came from nowhere.

'Christmas trees! People always need Christmas trees. Every year, they're lined up for sale. *Someone* must grow them. Let's put that down as number two.' I had no idea how much it would cost to grow them or how long it takes, but it was an idea.

2. Christmas tree plantation

'POO!' Juliette screamed.
I nearly jumped out of my skin.
'Sell poo!' she said. 'That's another sign we saw.'
'Oh, you mean manure,' I said. 'The dry stuff.'
I put it down.

3. Sell manure

I sat back and looked at the list. I couldn't imagine what Grandpa was going to say. It still all felt a bit hopeless but at least we'd made a start.

I had another idea. My friend Naomi in London loves going to car boot sales. I added that too.

4. Car boot sale

Grandpa will hate anything to do with car boot sales, I thought. But they bring in money and that's the main thing. Plus we need as many ideas as possible.

'Oh, and I almost forgot. We haven't put the first idea down yet.'

I quickly wrote it in.

5. Campsite

We hadn't really noticed the constant sound of chiselling until it suddenly stopped and all went quiet. We went outside and around the back of the campervan to sneak a peek at what Dave was working on.

'Is it a penguin?' Juliette asked.

'Nope.'

I looked at the big head shape that was beginning to emerge from the rounded piece of wood.

'Maybe an owl?' I asked.

'Yes! You got it!' said Dave. 'I must be doing something right.'

Juliette pulled a face.

'Well, I've got several more hours of work to do,' said Dave. 'I need to start chiselling the feathers and working on the eyes. I'll show you when it's more finished. How are the ideas coming by the way?'

'We've got a few,' I said. 'I'm not sure if there's a big one in there but we haven't given up yet.'

I think Juliette must have had enough for one day. She looked at Dave.

'I'm ready to do more work on my wooden doll,' she said.

Dave rummaged in his bag for a doll-shaped piece of wood and handed it to her.

'Try drawing the eyes on her face,' he said. 'Then find some thick twigs you can carve and add as arms.'

Juliette held up the piece of wood. 'It's called work in progress.'

'You sound like a real pro,' I said.

It was time for me to go back anyway. I stepped into the campervan to pick up my poster. When I reached for my phone, I saw it – five missed calls! All from Gabriel! Now I was the one banging my forehead with the heel of my hand. I'd left the phone on silent all afternoon and I hadn't even bothered to check it once.

Chapter 8

GABRIEL

On the way back to the farm, I stared at the mobile screen. I had promised to keep in touch but I'd been so busy with Juliette that I completely forgot. Now I felt bad. I rang him straight away but it was Mum who answered. She was at the hospital.

'Gabriel's having a rest,' she said. 'I'll get him to ring when he wakes up. Rob, one of his friends here, went home today. He's happy for him, of course, but sorry he can't go home too.'

I should have known Gabriel was down. Sometimes, we can each guess what the other is thinking or feeling. We call it 'twins' thought waves'. It's spooky but actually quite cool – and useful.

I'd just finished talking to Mum, when I saw Grandpa up ahead.

It's now or never, I suddenly thought.

'Grandpa, wait! I've got something to show you.' I waved my pieces of paper in the air.

He turned to me looking confused.

'I've got some new ideas for saving the farm. I thought you might be interested.'

Grandpa took the sheet from me and studied it. He mumbled a bit and every so often his eyebrows shot up.

He handed the sheet back.

'Abigay, I know you mean well,' he said. 'And these are all wonderful ideas but, it really is more complicated than that.'

He gave me a half-hearted pat on the shoulder then seemed lost for words. He paused for a minute, mumbled something and suddenly set off in the direction of the milking shed.

And that was that. So much for jam, eggs and manure. If none of those ideas are any good, what do we do?

I know what to do, I thought. I need to think of something really big!

Gabriel sounded tired and fed up when I spoke to him.

'Why didn't you answer my calls?' he said.

'Well, I was in the campervan with the Three Macs. It's like a jigsaw puzzle inside with so many cupboards and places for everything. They speak two languages, you know – English and French. Juliette's going to teach me some French.'

Gabriel was silent.

'You're not jealous, are you?' I said.

'Of course not,' said Gabriel. 'Why would I be jealous?'

'Oh my gosh! You *are* jealous! Well, if it's any help, it wasn't all fun. Juliette and I ended up slipping in the yard next to the cowshed and we got covered all over in cow poo!'

Gabriel spluttered and laughed out loud.

'Excuse me,' I said. 'It's not actually funny. Well, maybe it's just a little bit funny. OK! It's funny,' I admitted.

He finally stopped.

'What are they doing? Why are they camping on *our* farm? Isn't Easter too cold to camp anyway?' he asked.

'I don't know,' I said. 'Maybe it's a Canadian thing. Juliette said Canada is freezing in the winter so it must feel warm to them here.

'They've called their holiday "Looking for roots". They're going to Scotland after this, where Dave lived until he was ten years old. That's when he and his parents emigrated to Canada.

'Tammy's parents emigrated from France to Canada. I don't know if they are going to France as well.

'And you know what?' I said. 'Juliette doesn't go to school! She's home-schooled!'

'That sounds cool,' said Gabriel. 'I suppose that makes me hospital-schooled.'

'Grandpa's acting strangely again, by the way,' I said. 'He keeps disappearing off in the direction of the apple orchard. I'll let you know if I find out anything.'

I didn't mention my list of ideas or Grandpa's reaction. There was time enough for that later.

Gabriel sounded tired so we decided to finish the call.

'Don't forget to answer the phone next time,' he said.

After, I sent a quick text.

ME:

Why did the farmer drive the steamroller over his field?

GABRIEL:

I don't know. He wanted flat fields?

ME:

Wrong!
He wanted to grow mashed potatoes!

GABRIEL:

Oh! No! Your jokes are just getting worse. Catcha later!

Chapter 9

MIDNIGHT FOAL

'Wake up! Wake up!' It was Grandma.

I was fast asleep and it was the middle of the night. Now I was fully awake!

'Get dressed quickly!' she said. 'We're going to the lower field.'

Outside the moon was shining. There were inky, dark shadows everywhere. We had to be careful where we stepped. The metal of the gates felt cold as we climbed over them.

'Where are we going?' I asked Grandma.

'You'll soon see,' she said.

It was all very mysterious. I wished Gabriel was there.

At the field, I heard a soft noise, a gentle whinny. We came nearer and I saw Grandpa next to Beauty.

He put a hand up for us to stop.

'She needs help!' he whispered. 'She's delivered the foal but it can't breathe. Beauty needs to trust us now.'

I could hardly breathe myself.

'Abigay,' said Grandpa in a calm voice, 'hold the torch for me please.'

I moved closer and took the torch. I shone the beam of golden light to where he pointed.

He then turned to Grandma.

'As you know, it doesn't happen often but the birthing sack hasn't opened. This foal's in danger of drowning.'

I held the torch still as Grandpa put his finger through what looked like a slippery balloon. Suddenly, liquid spilled out and at that moment, I saw the little foal. It moved and came to life before our very eyes!

Beauty bent down and licked her newborn baby all over.

'Come away now!' whispered Grandpa. 'They need to be left alone for a bit.'

'Good work, Abigay!' said Grandma, giving me a squeeze.

'You won't see that often, Abigay,' said Grandpa. 'A mare will usually only give birth when no one is around but since it's her first I've been keeping an eye on Beauty.'

We looked back at Beauty's dark silhouette in the moonlight, moving gently around her foal. We stood as still as statues, each one of us lost in our own individual thoughts. No one wanted to speak and break the spell.

This is why I love being at the farm so much, I thought, more than anywhere else in the whole world. It's a place where *magical things happen*.

We slowly moved back over to Beauty and her foal.

'It's a boy!' Grandpa said. 'And he looks healthy.'

The tiny little thing tried to stand up on his long thin legs. He kept falling but Beauty was right beside him helping every time until, at last, he managed to stay standing.

He needed a drink. At first, he went to Beauty's front legs, then took a few more steps and went to the back legs where he found the right place! We kept still and quiet. I could hear him sucking.

'That first drink is full of goodness,' said Grandpa. 'It will give him strength.'

'Clever Beauty,' whispered Grandma. 'It's her firstborn but she knows exactly what to do. It's better for her and the foal if she does everything herself. We'll need to think of a name for the little fellow,' she said quietly.

'Let's ask Gabriel to think of a name,' I said.

'Yes, of course! We'll send him a photo.'

'It's time we got back to bed now,' said Grandpa, after we had waited quietly in the cool darkness for a while.

'We'll come back early in the morning.'

Back in my room, I couldn't sleep.

I know what I'll do, I thought. I'll send a message to Gabriel. He'll get it when he wakes up.

I reached for my phone and typed.

ME:

Hey Gabriel,
Mystery solved. I found out where Grandpa was going. And
it's good news!
Beauty's just had her foal...in the middle of the night...under
the moonlight!!...
and I got to see it!!!!
I sooo wish you could have been here.
But we all want YOU to choose
a name for him. Grandma's sending you a photo.

Chapter 10

GOOD NEWS

In the morning Gabriel replied:

GABRIEL:
Now I am jealous – for real!
I want to be there too.
But that's amazing!
Even the doctors are wondering why I'm so cheerful!
You say he was born under the moonlight.
Well, then he has to be called
MOONLIGHT!

After breakfast I heard Juliette's voice calling from the farmyard.

'Hellooooo! Abi! WHERE ARE YOU?'

Her eyes were shining with excitement as she burst into the kitchen.

'I've just heard about the foal. Your grandad told us! Why didn't you call me last night? Can we go and see him now?' She threw both arms in the air. (She's so dramatic!)

'It was too dark and too far to walk to your campervan,' I said. 'And anyway, Grandma kept it a secret until the last minute. But yes, we can go now!'

Juliette skipped all the way down to the lower field. She jumped up and over the two gates, hardly waiting for me to catch up. 'You're never going to be a gymnastics megastar,' she laughed.

I muttered under my breath. Sometimes, she's just so EXTRA. She's so sure she's going be a star – winning an Olympic Gold medal even. But I'm not sure what for. I'm pretty sure there's no Olympic medal for cartwheels, no matter how good they are.

We saw Grandpa when we reached the field.

'Let's all be quiet so as not to frighten the little fellow,' he said. 'I've been popping down to check on them. Look, he can walk already!'

It was so lovely to see the little foal walking around on his spindly legs. He discovered he could lift both legs off the ground and do a little jump.

'Gabriel's chosen a name for you,' I told him in a gentle voice. 'I hope you like it. It's Moonlight.'

'He can't answer,' Juliette giggled. She began to stare at Moonlight, pointing to his hooves. 'Is there something wrong with them?'

I didn't want to look. To me the little foal was JUST PERFECT! Trust Juliette to spoil a magical moment by talking too much and not thinking, I thought, but Grandpa didn't mind. He likes to explain about the farm and the animals.

'That's completely normal,' he said. 'His little hooves

have that soft covering to protect the mare during the birth. He doesn't need it anymore, so it's beginning to peel off.'

I dared myself to look.

Moonlight flopped down and lay flat on the grass. All of a sudden, he was tired and very soon fell asleep like a baby. The whole time Beauty kept guard over her precious foal.

'Auntie Rachel is so happy,' Grandpa said. 'Beauty was only a few months old when she brought her to the farm and now, she has her own little foal!'

Juliette pulled my sleeve. 'Let's go and collect eggs!' she said.

She isn't good at standing still and staring.

As we walked back up the hill, I thought about how my class at school loved the newborn donkey foal at the city farm and how we kept going back to see how much she had grown. I told Juliette about it.

'That's a lovely idea,' she said. 'I wish we had city farms like that in Canada.'

And that was the moment I had my next big idea!

As we approached the farmhouse, I heard what Grandpa calls 'a commotion'. Rosie the donkey was going hee-haw. The goats were bleating and the few cows left in the shed joined in with loud mooing. And all caused by Grandma running through the farmyard calling at the top of her voice.

'Gabriel's coming home for four days over Easter! They're letting him out tomorrow!'

I jumped in the air. 'The treatment must be working. This is the best news ever! I need to go home to London to be there with him. I just can't wait.'

Then I thought of an obvious question. 'When can someone drive me home?' I asked.

'Well, I expect…' Grandma started to say, but Juliette interrupted in a squeaky, excited voice.

'Oooh! London. Can I come too? I've always wanted to go to London! I want to see the queen and the palace and the Tower of London and the funny bridge that opens and closes.'

'Your parents will take you one day,' Grandma said quickly. 'Abigay is going to see Gabriel. He's been in a lot of pain but he's feeling a little better. Your parents will explain.'

Juliette looked disappointed, but seemed to understand and went back to the campervan.

That evening everybody was smiling. Grandma was chatting on the phone to Auntie Rachel who was going to pick me up in the morning and drive to London. Grandpa hummed as he walked across the yard. He looked back over his shoulder.

'Abigay,' he said, 'come and help with the milking.'

'Coming!' I yelled.

I've been in the milking parlour loads of times. We have to wear plastic aprons and put the milking teats onto the cows. Then we stand back and watch the milk being pumped into the container.

'I forgot how much milk each cow gives,' I said to Grandpa.

'Plenty,' said Grandpa. 'Problem is, we get so little money for it. We might just as well pour it straight down the sink!' He slapped his favourite cow on her hindquarters. 'But we'll carry on, won't we old girl. Until people come to their senses.'

Chapter 11

LONDON

The car journey home with Auntie Rachel seemed to take forever. We chatted and sang songs but mostly we drove in silence. I always know we are on our way back to London when we reach the deep cut through the white chalky hillside. From then on, we no longer see open fields stretching off into the distance or dense woods flashing by. Instead, it's just tree-lined roads for miles and miles. Usually I fall asleep, waking up with a jolt, but this time my head was so full of thoughts that I didn't sleep at all.

I kept thinking about my big idea. What if Gabriel didn't like it? I needed him to because so far NOBODY ELSE HAD THOUGHT OF ANYTHING.

Gradually, we began to see more bridges over the road and the tall blocks of flats and cranes rose up on the horizon. Soon, we were crossing the city through the traffic, the noise and the chaos. I couldn't wait to spend the weekend with Gabriel and I was looking forward to seeing Mum and Dad as well. We reached the massive roundabout before pulling into the quiet suburban roads. At LAST, we turned into our small street of red brick houses and spied Mum waiting by the edge of the pavement.

Auntie tooted the horn. Mum threw her arms round me as soon as I jumped out of the car. It felt *so* good.

The sun was shining and suddenly everything felt possible.

'Isn't it fantastic!' she said. 'A week ago, we never could have dreamt that Gabriel would be home for a visit.'

Mum was wearing her favourite apron, the one with puffins on it that Gabriel and I helped her to choose in Scotland – our last holiday together.

In the kitchen, chopped vegetables and jars of spice were everywhere. 'I'm getting everything ready for your dad's cooking tomorrow morning when Gabriel gets home from the hospital,' she said with a beaming smile.

'We're just having a simple supper tonight,' she said. 'Tomorrow Dad's cooking curry goat, Gabriel's favourite, followed by mangoes.'

She laughed her really happy laugh. I hadn't heard it for a long time and I'd missed it.

Everybody had so much to say that evening. But I wasn't really listening. I couldn't stop thinking about my idea to save Willowfield Farm and how I would explain it to Gabriel. Would it be fair to mention that we might lose the farm? I could tell him that Grandpa was looking for good ideas to make more money. And how I had a brilliant one that I needed to share with him, but IT NEEDED TO COME FROM BOTH OF US!

Chapter 12

HOSPITAL

When we reached Gabriel's ward, I quickly rubbed my hands with antiseptic gel from the pack on the wall, pressed the red button to open the door and walked in.

'Tell Gabriel we'll be along in a few minutes,' said Mum. 'We have to have a word with the doctor.'

Gabriel was sitting on his bed with a small bag beside him. I could see from his drooping shoulders that something was not quite right. I wanted to rush up and hug him, but I knew he would be horrified.

'We came as fast as we could,' I said. 'Is everything OK?'

'The doctors have just told me that I have to stay in the wheelchair all weekend,' he said. 'It's so stupid. They know I can move around on the crutches. I'm the ward's "crutches champion".'

'I know you are,' I said. I'd seen him in action. He was the only one on the ward with dark blue crutches – the same colour as his favourite football team.

'So why the wheelchair at home?' I asked.

'They say that I have to rest my joints.'

Gabriel seemed pretty miserable.

I looked over at the nurses' desk in the middle of the ward. Nurse Josephine was on duty. She's the one I know best. She was on the phone but gave a friendly wave anyway. I turned back to Gabriel and felt I needed to say something cheerful.

'You know Auntie Rachel has come to see you. She's waiting back at the house,' I said. 'We're all excited, so you'd better be too. We'll have a great Easter together. Anyway, you'll be nice and comfortable in the wheelchair and it's easier for us all to go out. We can take it in turns to push you.'

I tried my most cheerful grin. Gabriel didn't say anything more. He just looked a bit glum.

I caught sight of Mum, Dad, two senior nurses and two doctors disappearing into a side room.

'Do you know what they want to discuss?' I asked.

'The treatment isn't working,' he said. 'They've tried it for as long as they can. They think the best thing is for me to have the operation.'

I didn't know what to say. I'd used up all my "looking on the bright side" thoughts so I sat down on the bed next to Gabriel.

'Didn't someone say before that the treatment might not work? Maybe the operation is a better idea? Maybe that's good news?'

For a while Gabriel didn't say anything. Then he grinned.

'OK, Doctor Abigay,' he said. 'Perhaps you're right. Actually, that's what the doctor said this morning.'

I laughed – maybe a bit too loudly. People looked but I didn't care. Suddenly, we were both laughing together. It didn't make much sense but it felt way better.

Nurse Josephine came over to see if Gabriel had everything he needed. 'Your mum and dad will be back in a minute,' she said as she helped him into the wheelchair.

'And then you'll be off. It's good to see you two together again. Make sure you get plenty of Easter eggs and have a great family party. I hear your aunt is here as well. Aren't you the VIP!'

While we were waiting, I looked round the ward. There was a new boy in a bay near the nurses' desk. He looked quite young. I wandered over.

'Hello. I'm Abigay, Gabriel's twin,' I smiled. 'Our grandma says we're like two peas in a pod. Except he's just a bit darker than me and his hair's shorter.'

The boy just gave a weak smile.

'He can't speak English,' said Gabriel. 'His family doesn't either – just a big cousin who comes in to translate what the nurses and doctors say.'

At that moment, Mum and Dad came back.

'Everything's OK for the weekend,' Mum said.

'So can we go?' I asked. 'I've got so many photos to show Gabriel and some very important things to discuss.'

Chapter 13

HOME

The hospital corridor felt long as I pushed Gabriel in the wheelchair.

'If I had a chair with big wheels, then I could wheel myself,' he grumbled.

'Just relax,' I said, not wanting to argue. 'We're going home.' I went fast and then slow, then fast again to make him laugh.

'Stop mucking around,' said Gabriel.

At last, we came out into the bright sunshine. Gabriel didn't want Dad to help him as he climbed into the back of the car. I couldn't help noticing how slowly he moved.

Gabriel went quiet again. Isn't he excited about coming home? I wondered.

'Have you heard from Rob?' I asked.

Gabriel nodded.

'Oh, I do have news,' Gabriel suddenly said.

'Really?' I said. 'What is it?'

'An artist is coming to do a project with us at the

Activity Centre. There's going to be a public display of art by the kids so people can see what we do at the centre. They're hoping people with loads of money will give some to the hospital, I guess.'

'Cool! Maybe I could show some pictures too,' I said.

'Yeah. Maybe. I'll ask,' said Gabriel. 'It should be fine, since you've been to the centre.'

'I could draw Moonlight,' I said. 'What are you going to do?'

Gabriel shrugged his shoulders.

'Don't know yet. I'll try a few things.'

At home, we have a small downstairs room used for coats and boots and bikes. Over the last months, it's been Gabriel's bedroom because he was limping and couldn't get upstairs. Mum wheeled him in and I followed. He looked round the room, at his football posters and his Star Wars lego models. 'I've got so much to tell you about the farm,' I said, '*and* I've got loads of photos of Moonlight to show you!'

But Gabriel wasn't listening.

'Let's go in the kitchen,' he said to Mum.

'Look,' I said, 'Mum has put one of the signs you made on the fridge. The one saying "I'll be back".' Gabriel's calligraphy is amazing! He learnt it at the Activity Centre and now he practises, all the time.

He looked at the carrots, garlic, onions and curry powder.

'Are we having Dad's special?' he asked. 'We never have anything like that at the hospital.'

I so wanted to talk to Gabriel in private about the farm but every time I tried, somebody else started to chat with him. First it was Auntie Rachel, then Mum and Dad, *then even the neighbours popped in*!

By the end of the evening, Gabriel couldn't keep his eyes open. Mum decided to send him to bed early. It wasn't fair. I hadn't had a single chance to talk to him about the one thing that *really* mattered.

I escaped to my bedroom and shut the door. I decided that I wasn't going to talk to anyone else until I got to talk to Gabriel!

A few minutes later, Mum came up. 'Are you upset?' she asked. She stayed with me for ages and stroked my forehead. It felt nice and comforting. We didn't say anything for a long time.

'I know it's hard,' she said eventually, 'but you know, the doctors and nurses are very hopeful about Gabriel's recovery after the operation. It's definitely the best option.'

'I know,' I said, 'but you don't understand! Nobody does. Gabriel and I need time together. We've got something important to talk about.'

Mum leaned back against my pillow. She looked so tired. Something in my head said: Don't tell her that Willowfield Farm might be sold. She has enough to worry about.

Thoughts were circling in my head like a washing machine spinning round.

Mum gave me a big hug and plumped up the pillow behind me. She put her arm around my shoulders.

'I can't imagine what you plan to cook up with Gabriel but I promise you can have as much time together as you want tomorrow morning, as long as everyone else has time with him in the afternoon. How does that sound?'

'Good,' I said.

'So that's agreed then,' said Mum and she kissed me on the forehead.

I snuggled down into the covers and closed my eyes.

Finally, I thought. I'll get to talk to Gabriel about saving Willowfield Farm. I just *had* to convince him about my big idea.

We've always done everything together. And that was what we'll do this time!

TWINS TO THE RESCUE!

Chapter 14

MAKING PLANS

ABIGAY

GABRIEL

I was up hours before Gabriel. When I heard him rustle around in bed, I quietly tapped on his door and entered the room. I sat on the bed for a while and then I started to tell him everything.

I spoke to him about the small farmers having meetings and discussing ways they could earn more money and I talked about how Grandpa met with Mr King.

'And Christopher had to come as well,' I said with a groan.

Gabriel shook his head in disbelief.

'And in the milking parlour, Grandpa told me we don't get a good price for the milk. He said "we might as well pour the milk down the sink".'

Gabriel stared at me. 'Did he ACTUALLY say that? This is awful. It's just not fair!'

Then I told him about the farmer in the newspaper who sold his farm.

Gabriel gasped. 'That's terrible! We mustn't let that happen to Willowfield.'

I began to talk faster. 'Grandma told me about the ideas people had come up with and how Grandpa said NO to all of them.' I talked about the list that Juliette and I had written.

'I don't understand why Grandpa says no to *everything*,' Gabriel said.

'Me neither,' I said. 'But then I had a REALLY BIG IDEA, the night Moonlight was born, and I've been waiting *and waiting* to talk to you about it.'

'So what are you waiting for?' said Gabriel. 'Let's hear it.'

'Well, we should open the farm for people to visit – like the city farm. Schools and families would pay to see a real working farm. Children could even help out.'

Gabriel smiled a huge smile – the first big happy smile I had seen all weekend. 'That's a great idea!' he said.

We talked about going to the city farm with our primary school.

'The best thing is feeding the animals,' Gabriel said.

We had a good laugh about the pot-bellied pig and the goats that leapt up the steep railway embankment.

'There's no railway embankment at Willowfield,' Gabriel said, which gave me another good idea – a way of keeping goats happy.

'We could build them their own goat mountain out of rocks and boulders.'

I thought for a moment. 'You know what else is always popular. It's the cuddle barn where children can stroke baby guinea pigs, baby rabbits and other animals.'

So we both decided that SOMETHING MUST BE DONE.

'We should draw up a plan,' said Gabriel.

He found some cream-coloured card and wrote slowly and carefully.

Proposal
WILLOWFIELD OPEN FARM
for schools and families
by
Abigay and Gabriel Miller

I noticed that writing seemed to make him tired.

'Tell you what, let's scribble our ideas on a piece of rough paper and I'll copy them out later in my best writing,' I suggested. I was glad that Gabriel was as excited as I was about the idea.

Anything that takes his mind off his illness has got to be a good thing, I thought.

Next, I would have to find a way to talk to Grandma and Grandpa about our proposal!

When Auntie Rachel and I reached Willowfield farm, before I could sit down in peace and start copying out the notes, Juliette came charging up the path and banged on the kitchen door.

'You're back!' she said. 'I missed you!' Her eyes were shining and she handed me a beautiful daisy chain. 'I made this for you! It took ages! I hope you like it!'

I put it on my head. 'Thanks!' I said. 'I feel like a princess!'

Juliette laughed and then rushed off a million questions: 'How is Gabriel? What did you do together? Did you tell him about me? Is he feeling better?'

She went on and on. In the end, the only thing to do was to go outside and play with her. We went on the swing and then sat on a bench in the farm garden.

When Juliette finally went to her campervan for a meal, I could *at last* get down to writing out our notes.

I sat down and started to copy out the rough notes in my best handwriting.

Why an Open Farm?

To make enough money to keep the farm going for years to come.

Things for children to see and enjoy

- Baby animals, like guinea pigs, little chicks, ducklings, rabbits
- Bottle feeding calves and lambs
- Brooms for children to help with sweeping
- Bags of food for children to feed chickens and pigs
- Looking at newborn animals, like Moonlight
- Collecting eggs

What we Need:

1. A sitting area with benches for picnics

2. Welly boots of all different sizes
3. Children's toilets
4. Rules about touching farm animals and washing hands
5. Figures and information (teachers LOVE this kind of thing)
6. Worksheets with drawing paper, pencils and felt tips for children to draw

What's Next

Discussion with Auntie Rachel for ideas on how to run our project.
Signed: Abigay and Gabriel.

All I needed to do now was to show it to Grandma and Grandpa – that would be the difficult bit…

Chapter 15

PROPOSAL

We were in the kitchen after the evening meal. I love Grandma and Grandpa's kitchen. It's so cosy and different from the one at home with its all-white cupboards. At the farm, there's always a bright cloth on the table and lots of chairs. There's a bright red cooker and a copper kettle.

Gabriel and I often help polish the copper kettle. It's a messy job but it's fun. Gabriel pretends he doesn't like doing it much but always tries to make his side of the kettle shine more than mine.

The kitchen dresser has blue and white plates arranged standing up so you can see the patterns. Underneath there's a row of funny mugs. Two of them are special mugs we brought back from Jamaica when we went to visit our other grandparents – Dad's parents. Gabriel likes the mug with a picture of a beautiful hummingbird and I like the one with a pretty blue flower. It's the national flower of Jamaica. This time the mug with the beautiful picture of a hummingbird was still on the shelf.

I felt my heart beating fast and a banging in my ears. But this was something that had to be done.

I slipped out of the kitchen to get the proposal from where I left it – on top of the washing machine outside in the corridor.

I came back and stood with the paper in my hand, ready for my big moment, but nobody was looking at me. I didn't move. I just stood there.

Grandma glanced over. She must have seen the expression on my face. She turned towards me.

'Is something bothering you?' she said.

Her words nearly made me choke. I heard my words tumbling out.

'There's something important I want to talk about,' I said. 'It's something Gabriel and I want to show you.'

I stopped. The next bit was difficult. I took a deep breath.

'I told Gabriel that the farm isn't making enough money from the milk and that lots of farmers are selling up. And I know it's true, 'cos I saw the article about it in the newspaper...'

Grandma and Grandpa didn't say anything so I carried on.

'I didn't want to upset Gabriel while he's ill, but I just had to share my idea with him. Now we both think the same. WE want to keep the farm going FOREVER. And we've got a plan!'

I stopped and took a deep breath.

'Grandpa didn't like any of the ideas people thought of before, but we've written down our idea and we want you to think about it.'

I put the proposal on the table. Grandma and Grandpa hesitated, then moved their chairs so that they could both read it together.

Tick Tock! Tick Tock! went the kitchen clock as they read. Nobody spoke. I hardly dared to breathe.

I didn't know what Grandma and Grandpa would say. I remembered how horrified Gabriel had been when I told him about the problems with the farm.

I told myself, I really hope Grandma and Grandpa are pleased with the plan. They can't say no to trying to save the farm. They just can't!

It seemed like ages before Grandpa let out the deep sigh. It was the sigh of a man who'd lost his patience. What I heard next was something I never expected to hear, something I never want to hear ever again. Grandma put her hand on Grandpa's wrist and whispered something in his ear, but he slowly moved it aside. He put both hands on the table and pushed his chair back, making a horrible scraping noise that hurt my ears. He heaved himself up to a standing position, then spoke in a loud voice that I've only ever heard him use once before at the cattle market.

'I've told you before this isn't a problem for children! This is a grown-up's problem! How you two can ever imagine you can solve the problems of a farm is beyond me! It's absolutely ridiculous! And let's be clear! No one's going to turn my farm into a playground! This is a working farm! It's not a school project!'

I'd never seen Grandpa like this. I wanted to cover my ears. I watched in horror as he let our proposal drop back onto the table and headed for the door. As he stormed out into the farmyard I could still hear him shouting.

'I've been working this farm for nigh on fifty years and no one has ever told me how to do my job! Now I'm expected to let two children tell me how to run things!'

Tears began to prickle my eyes. Grandma looked almost as shocked as I was and I could see she didn't know what to do. She started to talk in a soothing voice but I couldn't take any more.

'Just don't say *anything*!' I shouted. 'You don't UNDERSTAND! NOBODY DOES!'

Big sobs began to shake my body. I ran out of the kitchen and upstairs to my bedroom. I threw myself on the bed and buried my head under the pillow. My tears felt hot and my head began to ache.

How could I have been *so* silly! Why *would* Grandpa listen when he had refused to listen to anybody else. And why would a grown-up listen to children with their silly plan anyway. How could I have been *so* stupid.

I wasn't going to talk to ANYONE anymore about the farm. I was done trying to help.

On the bedside table the phone vibrated. I glanced at it and felt a cold chill run through me – MISSED CALL FROM GABRIEL! I had completely forgotten that he was waiting to hear how things went. I turned the phone off. I had missed calls from him before, but this was the first time *ever* that I didn't respond.

There was a little tap on the door.

I knew it was Grandma. I squeezed my eyes shut and pretended to be asleep until I heard the door close softly again. Very soon I was fast asleep for real.

Chapter 16

THE BARN

When I woke up, I wasn't upset anymore – I was angry.
I knew I had two problems:

1. What to say to Gabriel?
2. What to do about our plan?

When Gabriel's in hospital, it's never easy to know when
to ring. Nurses and doctors are often in his room and he's
not always free to talk. I was angry about Grandpa refusing
to listen and I wanted Gabriel to feel angry too. It was
probably not a good idea to upset him but I just didn't care.

I dialled the number and waited for him to reply. He
didn't answer which was probably for the best. I sent him a
text instead.

ME:

Sorry I didn't call you yesterday.
Any news about the date of your operation?

I started to think about Problem Number Two: What to do about our plan?

It was after breakfast, so hopefully Grandpa would be out on the farm somewhere out of the way.

Grandma wasn't around either when I reached the kitchen so I helped myself to cereal, fruit and two pieces of toast. Soon I was ready to go outside. I had made up my mind. I wasn't going to give up without a fight!

I was walking round the yard, kicking dry bits of mud, having a think, when I saw Dave. He was at the water tap filling up a big plastic container.

'Hey there!' he said. 'How are your plans going?' It was just a polite question but he caught me off guard.

'Great!' I lied. 'Gabriel and I worked out something really BIG, just like you said.'

'Good for you,' said Dave. 'Keep on with your dream, young warrior girl!'

I wandered into the farm garden and headed for the new swing.

Yeah right, I thought. It's easy for Dave to say 'keep on with your dream'.

I sat on the swing and moved slowly backwards and forwards. I didn't realise how tightly I was gripping the rope and my fingers began to ache. Just like my brain was aching. How come my silent-but-always-friendly Grandpa had suddenly turned into King of the Grumps who wouldn't listen to anybody – not even me?

Backwards and forwards. Backwards and forwards. Suddenly, I had AN IDEA! I sprang off the swing and hurried back to the farmyard. I was surprised to see Dave still there. He was talking to Grandma but neither of them saw me. Good! I didn't need them!

I carried on up the slope to the big barn. I didn't know if I would be able to open the door by myself but I HAD TO! If nobody was going to help with the proposal, then I would just have to make a start by myself! I wasn't used to doing things without Gabriel, but this time it was all down to me.

I pushed hard at the heavy wooden door and slowly, slowly managed to open it. It made a loud creaking noise. Nobody came to see what I was doing and I was soon inside.

The barn was quite dark and smelled dusty. I looked up to the high arched roof. There were windowpanes up there that let some light in and slowly my eyes got used to the gloom. I could see bits of dust dancing in the bright shafts that shone down from above.

I looked at the stacked-up bales of straw. Last summer, on a very wet day, Gabriel and I played inside this barn and made hidey-holes between the square bales. Now I had a more serious mission. It involved moving bales onto the barn floor. I chose the ones nearest the bottom that didn't have too many resting on them. It wasn't easy to pull them out but bit by bit I managed.

Soon, I had eight large bales arranged in a semicircle. My hands were scratched and sore but I managed to drag out one more and placed it facing the others. I sat down on the last one. For a long time, I imagined myself as a teacher talking to a class of kids sitting on the bales. I acted out passing round tiny chicks to each child.

I remembered how Grandma showed me how to make a cup with your hand for a chick or a little animal to sit in. If you partly cover it with your other hand, the chick will feel safe and won't get squashed.

Children visiting our Open Farm will love feeling them and looking at their little bodies, I thought. They'll learn about nature and living things, just like at the city farm.

'Right!' I said to myself, looking round the barn. Things were scattered everywhere.

'Time to start the clear-up!'

I made my way to the lower end of the barn.

It was hard to know where to begin. There were wooden boxes and bits of corrugated iron lying all over the floor. I picked them up and put them along the side wall, making quite a big space in the middle of the floor. It was already starting to look better.

The more I cleared, the more I discovered, including old farm tools and machinery. I recognised a wooden plough in among the long-handled scythes, the old pitchforks and the wide wooden hay rakes.

These can all be used to create a display, I thought. That way, visitors can learn about farming in the old days.

Suddenly, more light flooded into the barn. That's when I noticed Grandma in her blue dungarees by a side door that I had forgotten about.

How long has she been here? I wondered.

'Where to begin,' Grandma was saying to herself. 'I think I'll start by moving some of these old plastic buckets up here.'

We worked away quietly at different ends of the barn. After a while, I couldn't hear her moving. I peeped and saw her sitting quietly on the teacher's straw bale. I wished I knew what she was thinking.

All of a sudden, we were brought back to the present by a loud shriek.

'I've found you. You're here!'

It was Juliette – nobody else could produce a shriek like that! She bounced into the barn like an overexcited puppy.

'Can I help?' Juliette yelled, which was the last thing I wanted to hear. What I wanted was a bit of peace and quiet for Grandma and me to work ALONE without Juliette butting in as usual. But it was no good.

Grandma answered for me. 'Great idea!' she said. 'Just don't move anything heavy.'

Juliette's idea of tidying was crazy. She found an old broom and started sweeping like mad. She made so much dust rise in the air that it got into my eyes, nose and throat and I started coughing.

As I moved away from her as fast and as far as I could, I stumbled over a pile of old, brown newspapers. That's when I noticed a strange shape on the barn floor where they had been stacked. It was as if someone had drawn a perfect square in the hard earth. I tapped it. It sounded like metal. I bent down and felt all round the edges. It was a square and looked as if it had been buried right into the earth.

'Grandma!' I called. 'There's something buried in the floor and it's hard to move. Can you help?'

Juliette came running. 'Is it treasure?' she asked. Her eyes were shining. 'If it is, then you can sell it and be rich and the farm will be saved and we'll all live happily ever after!'

Grandma came over and peered at the metal square. She reached for a small trowel and slowly loosened the soil round the edges. Bit by bit, she managed to ease out a dusty metal box. We tried to open it, but it wouldn't budge.

'Come,' said Grandma. 'Let's go into the kitchen and figure out how to get this thing open!'

Juliette walked even faster than usual towards the farm house.

'Hurry!' she said. 'I can't wait to see what's inside.'

Grandma followed slowly with a puzzled expression on her face.

'What can this be? It's too small and light to be an unexploded World War Two bomb,' she muttered. 'We should be grateful for that at least.'

Juliette was bouncing up and down like a wound-up clockwork toy when we reached the kitchen.

'So let's open it NOW!' Juliette said.

'Hold on a minute!' Grandma said as she covered the

table with newspaper. She turned the tin over and examined the lid.

I could hear things shifting around inside.

'Mmm! This still won't budge,' she said. 'We're going to need some penetrating oil.'

Grandma disappeared into the boot room by the back door. It was full of rows of boots, untidy shelves stacked with bottles and tins above the white sink and draining board, and caps and waterproofs all hanging in a higgledy-piggledy way.

'It'll be a miracle if Grandma finds anything in there,' I said to Juliette.

But miraculously, Grandma reappeared seconds later holding the spray can up high. She sprayed around the lid and hinges.

'And now,' she said, 'we wait!'

As we waited, I looked shyly at Grandma. I felt bad about yesterday and how I had treated her.

'Grandma,' I said quietly. 'I'm sorry about yesterday.'

She gave a little smile and squeezed my hand gently.

'It's OK,' she whispered.

'Is it ready yet?' Juliette asked for about the sixth time.

Grandma leaned forward and tried opening the tin. The lid moved a bit.

'It's coming!' she called out. And then it was open.

Juliette and I bumped heads as we both bent closer to peer inside. We could see a jumble of old objects, newspaper cuttings and photos.

'There's nothing here that looks like treasure,' said Juliette disappointed.

'Why would somebody bury these things?' I asked

Grandma. I picked up a bundle of photographs, then looked closer at the one on the top of the pile.

'Look! That boy looks a bit like Grandpa. Is it him?'

Grandma took her glasses off to study the photo.

'Why yes! I think you're right!' she said.

'You know what,' she said, 'there's time enough to figure it all out later.' She put everything back carefully, squeezed the lid shut and left the mysterious box on the table.

'We can ask Grandpa when he decides to behave himself,' said Grandma.

Juliette was suddenly bored.

'I think I'm going to work on my doll sculpture,' she said.

'And I'm going upstairs,' I said. 'I promised Gabriel I would send him a message.'

Chapter 17

GRANDPA

The sun was high when Grandpa looked at his watch. Nearly eleven o'clock – coffee time. He had been up since six o'clock as usual, but what wasn't usual was him avoiding Grandma and Abigay. He had never been cross with Abigay before. He felt his shoulders droop and he had to take deep breaths. He remembered the evening before. Of course, he had every right to protest!

Grandpa listened carefully as he walked past the kitchen window. No sound of the kettle boiling.

'They're probably avoiding me too,' he said partly to himself and partly to the two farm cats stretched out in the sunshine.

The ginger one looked up, ready to leap off the wall at any moment. They were like that, the farm cats. You couldn't stroke them like indoor cats. They were too independent. They had their own places to stay and they found their own food. They regarded the farm as theirs.

The white cat looked far too comfortable to move.

'I'm sure they thought I was harsh,' said Grandpa. He sat down on the bench beside the wall and addressed both cats. 'But what do they know? It's not easy saving a small farm from financial disaster.'

Neither cat looked impressed. Grandpa shrugged his shoulders and slipped into the kitchen. He passed the range and headed straight for the electric kettle. He would make a coffee as quickly as possible and disappear before anyone arrived.

He loved it when the twins came to stay. They were lively and enthusiastic and their love of the animals made him feel young again. That was before Gabriel's long battle with his painful hip. It had been a worrying time for everyone – a sick grandchild and a failing farm. And now, to make matters worse, the twins had started all this nonsense with their proposal!

How on earth was he supposed to react to that? He knew *he* was right, even though it made everyone else upset.

He took his mug of coffee to the table, then noticed the square metal box. There was something about it that made him stop and sit down slowly.

The rust and the dirt hid something that was faintly familiar.

'Why I remember this!' he said suddenly. 'It's my old time capsule, the one that's supposed to stay buried for 100 years. What's it doing here on the kitchen table?'

He carefully opened the lid. It wasn't easy with his coarse weather-beaten hands. He brought out the long-forgotten objects and laid them carefully on the wooden surface:

A small bag of marbles – blue and grey and silvery
A large, metal door key
A bronze medallion from the harness of a working horse
Some predecimal coins
A model tractor
A rosette
Newspaper cuttings
Photographs
A gold box
An earring with an agate stone

He smiled to himself as he remembered walking along the pebbly beaches where his relatives had lived. His mother had always been able to pick out the semi-precious stones. They shone and glinted in the sun. As a short little boy he thought that as he was much closer to the pebbles, *he* should be able to find them, but it was always his mother who spotted them first. She would take them to the shop and get small bits of money in exchange. It was on the beach that they had found the cream-coloured agate stones that were made into earrings. When she lost one of them, she put the other in the memory tin.

He lifted out a small, gold box and stroked its smooth surface. 'I've given up smoking, so you might as well put that in too,' his dear old dad had said. 'I wonder what the farm will look like in 100 years when this is opened!' he'd added with that big laugh of his.

He unearthed three articles about England's triumphant World Cup win in 1966 and remembered all the excitement at the time.

The objects roused memories in Grandpa, but it was the

bundle of photos that made so many more come flooding back.

He was so far away in his thoughts that he didn't hear boots being scraped on the kitchen mat. Grandma was at the door!

Chapter 18

BEDROOM

I lay on my bed and stared at the ceiling. It was old and there were cracks in the dark brown beams. For a while, all I could hear was the distant sound of a duck quacking, then loud mooing from the three cows that were still in the cowshed. Then I heard the scrunch of car tyres. I could hear the postlady talking to Grandma. Grandma must have taken the post into the kitchen then, as I heard the door close with its familiar creak.

I slowly became aware of a fly buzzing around the room, then another different buzzing from the bedside table. My phone. I glanced at it. That would be Gabriel still waiting for information about our grand proposal. I didn't answer. I felt awful but what could I tell him? Every time I went to message him, I stopped myself. It was bad enough waiting for an operation for who knows when and then to be told that our dear old grandpa was angry with us.

The phone went quiet. Shortly after, the sound of the

buzzing fly faded as it flew out the open window into the bright sunshine.

Then another familiar noise high overhead. It was an old-fashioned plane with a propeller and flat, wide wings. It belonged to Mr King, Christopher's dad.

It always annoyed Grandpa when he heard it. I could hear his voice in my head now. 'Where there's an abundance of muck, there's brass – always money,' he'd grumble. 'But it doesn't work for us small farmers!'

The strange thing was, I liked the loud purring sound of the engine in the sky. For me, it was one of the sounds of spring and summer at the farm. It made me feel quite sleepy.

I was woken from my half-dreaming by raised voices. It took me a while to realise that it was Grandma and Grandpa. They were doing something they never, ever did – they were arguing. They sometimes bickered it's true, but this was different. This was a proper argument. This was serious. This was BIG.

I could pick out words like 'Fred King' and 'after this place for years'. Then, even LOUDER, 'You can't argue with figures!' The voices went quiet again. For a while, I couldn't make out much, until Grandma's voice came over loud and clear.

'Months!' she shouted. 'That's how long I've had to endure that piece of corrugated metal flapping on the shed roof!'

Now Grandpa was shouting again, '...not made of money...won't be told...people should come to their senses...'

Just when I thought the argument was over, Grandma was at it again.

'Edward Bertram Woolgar, just remember this is not your farm…this is *our* farm…and don't you forget it…'

Now Grandma was shouting so loudly, I could hear EVERYTHING!

'You can remember things when it suits you, but when it comes to how things were in the old days, suddenly your memory's not so good. Look at those photos. Your father and grandfather never gave up. They moved with the times. You did too. So what's different now?!'

I wanted to cover my ears but instead I strained to hear more. Grandpa sounded a bit quieter…

'They're young! They don't understand.'

Grandma continued at full volume. 'That poor girl… desperately wanted to help…you broke her heart…'

My face flushed hot red when I realised it was me they were talking about. I felt like hiding away and not coming out – ever!

But things seemed to calm down then. They were still talking but it wasn't an argument anymore. I didn't dare leave my bedroom.

After what seemed forever, there was a gentle tap, tap, tap.

'Abigay,' – it was Grandma calling quietly from behind the door – 'can you come down for a minute? Grandpa has something he wants to say. I'll join you both in a bit.'

I made my way downstairs and entered the kitchen carefully. Grandpa was sitting quietly at the table with the tin box in front of him. There was a chair pulled out next to him that was clearly for me. I sat down and waited. The ginger farm cat peered in the window before darting off who knows where.

Neither of us spoke. I heard the constant whooshing of the dishwasher and stared at the numbers counting down on the display panel.

I wondered whether Grandpa really did have something to say to me, when he cleared his throat and glanced at me awkwardly.

'1966,' he said softly, pointing to the mysterious box and the objects laid out around it. 'That's when we did these.'

I waited.

'It's all about history, you know,' he said eventually.

Another pause.

'I was about your age when our teacher got us to do them – time capsules she said they were.

'"Bury things that mean something to you," she said. "Then when people open them in 100 years, they'll know all about you and the times you lived in."

'On the lids we wrote "Do NOT Open until 2066". You can't see the writing anymore. I think I must have used the wrong kind of ink.

'But you know what? Now is as good a time as any. Maybe, it's important for you and Gabriel to learn about the old days and the old ways – and anyway, we can always bury it again afterwards.'

He shifted around and looked at me directly. I could see he wasn't angry anymore but there was a sadness in his eyes.

'You and I are not so different, girl,' he said. 'You do know that, don't you?

'A long time ago, I was young too. What I'm trying to say is…' He paused.

'Abigay, I think I owe you a big apology.'

Chapter 19

TIME CAPSULE

'Let me tell you, Abigay, why I put these things in the time capsule,' said Grandpa. He picked up the small bag of marbles.

'In those days, we used to have a craze for playing ringers in the playground. The big ones are the shooters. The rest are either aggies or alleys but mostly cat's eyes. By 1966 I'd outgrown these. That's why all my favourites are in here.'

He reached for a handful of strange coins of different shapes and sizes. 'I thought that people with metal detectors, archaeologists and the like, would get really excited by these!' he said with a chuckle.

'My father said I should put this in,' he said, picking up a red rosette. 'I was only eleven years old, when I won my first prize for a lamb. I hand-reared it as the mother had twins and couldn't feed both of them herself. He said it would represent my many years of attendance at farm shows.'

Grandpa talked about the horse brass, the earring, the cigarette case...

I pointed at the tractor.

'How could you bear to put that in?' I said. 'My friend Naomi's dad collects models like these – it's beautiful!'

'Well, there's a reason,' Grandpa said. 'I was about your age. My father had at last allowed me to drive the farm tractor, so in my mind, I had outgrown my toys. By then, I was a real farmer.'

He handed me a large metal key with a swirly pattern at the top. 'I remember finding this in an old outhouse that my father rebuilt.' He said, 'It's the original key to the farmhouse. Having a key to the door was a very significant thing – especially in those days.

'Now take a look at this.' Grandpa was having a long hard look at a brown and white, slightly blurred photo he had picked from the pile. The edges were tattered. It was a picture of a man standing in front of the farmhouse. He had long leather boots nearly up to his knees, an open shirt and a big hat. He looked happy, was smoking a pipe and pointing in the direction of the front door. You could tell it was Willowfield even though it looked very different. There was no porch by the front door and no rose or pear tree climbing up the walls. The windows looked rickety.

'That man was *my* grandfather,' said Grandpa. 'Of course I didn't know him when he was a young man like that, but he often told me how he saved up over the years to buy this farm. He had been renting it and at last, on the very day this photo was taken, he became the owner. He now possessed the key to the door – this very key! – and with it, the farmhouse and all the surrounding land. It was the proudest day of his life!'

I peered at the next photo. There were so many people

in the field, young and old, men, women and children. Some were sitting on the ground in family groups having picnics. There were also dogs and even rabbits escaping from men with shotguns. About half the cornfield had been cut, but some men were still busy cutting the last bit in the middle.

'Just think of that!' said Grandpa. 'All those workers were involved – nearly half the village.'

He remembered something else. 'My grandfather always told me about the changes he made once the farm was his. Then there were all the changes my own dad made when he was a young farmer. He introduced the combine harvester, you know. Nowadays one person can cut all the corn – what used to be the job of all those people in the photo! – then all he needed was a couple of people in tractors to haul the trailers. Moving with the times, he called it. When it was my turn, I had lots of ideas too – not all of them well received but we always listened to each other and we always tried to improve things. And your grandmother too when she came to live at the farm. Somehow, along the way, I've forgotten all of that…that is, until now.'

Grandpa took another one of his long pauses.

'Of course, we'll continue to do what we do here at the farm but that's not to say we can't adapt or try new things. I know your mother's heart is in her medical research and your dad's too. And that's important work. Your parents are never going to run the farm but Abigay, you and Gabriel are the next generation and yes, we do want the farm to be there for you! Of course, you're going to have your own ideas. And of course, we should listen to you too. So, let's have a proper look at these plans of yours.'

When I heard these words, I felt so proud, not just of myself and Gabriel, but of my grandpa who was finally learning to change. I was so happy to have him back. I reached over and I hugged him so, so hard.

'Is there room for one more?' a voice said. It was Grandma. How long had she been standing there listening?

'But remember, Abigay,' said Grandpa, 'it won't be easy. We need to discuss it with the bank manager in order to apply for a loan, draw up a business plan, work out the cost, carry out a feasibility study – he's going to want to see all of that.'

I nodded in agreement.

After that, there was just one more thing to do.

Chapter 20

VIDEO CALL

It felt strange seeing Gabriel's beaming face on the computer when we told him the news. I couldn't believe we managed to do a video call on Grandma's old computer.

His face lit up even more as we showed him object after object from the time capsule. I zoomed in on the photo of the farmhouse. He drew in a deep breath.

'That's amazing!' he said. 'It looked so different in the old days! They've added bits at the side of the house since then, haven't they, Grandpa?' He sounded really loud and not at all like a person in pain.

'Those photos are brilliant – I love the ones from the harvest! You know, we can blow these pictures up really big and have them mounted on display boards – they can do that nowadays. Then we can exhibit them next to all the old farm tools and machinery for the Open Farm.'

He paused, then said in a cheeky voice, 'Grandpa, how about alpacas?'

It wasn't the first time Gabriel had tried to convince

Grandpa and Grandma to keep alpacas. 'They look so gentle and interesting and have all different colours. People would love to see them!'

'You and your alpacas,' Grandpa said trying not to smile. 'Well, we want to show traditional British farming, but I suppose there's no reason we can't squeeze in a few alpacas.'

'And we could have tractor rides round the farm for kids and people who can't walk,' said Gabriel. 'They could sit in a trailer and you could tell them all about the crops and animals and everything.'

This time Grandpa had to laugh.

'We'll see,' he said. 'Just don't get overexcited, lad. You'll need all your strength for your operation. You need to concentrate on getting better!'

Later, I wandered out into the farm. I was excited about all that happened but I also needed time alone to think – luckily Juliette was nowhere to be seen.

I spent a while looking at the little piglets suckling, then turned to the goats and their two little kids. They always made me smile. I went to see my old friend Rosie the donkey. As I patted her and felt her thick grey fur, I told her the brilliant news.

I knew she couldn't understand me, but Rosie tilted her head upwards and let out a huge braying noise – hee-haw… hee-haw – that echoed loudly all around the farmyard!

Chapter 21

DAD

I had everything packed early on the Saturday. It was time to go home and back to school. I was going to miss Willowfield like crazy but I would get to see Gabriel.
Dad didn't arrive until the middle of the morning.

'It was a long slow drive today,' he said. 'What I need now is a nice strong coffee.'

Grandma was way ahead of him. She handed him a steaming mug, poured juice for me and Juliette and gave us each a big piece of jam sponge cake. We all sat on the low wall outside the kitchen.

'Hello Abigay's dad!' Juliette said. 'We all want to hear how Gabriel is.'

Everyone started talking at once.

'Stop!' Dad laughed and clapped his hands. Then he became more serious. 'Well, Gabriel is still in pain but he's keeping his spirits up until we get a date for the operation and we should all do the same. So be patient and try not to worry. The doctors are confident the operation will be a success.'

Nobody spoke after that. I munched my piece of cake.

'Listen!' Dad said, putting his hands behind his ears. 'The beautiful sound of silence!'

He was right. It can be quiet sometimes when the animals are not making a noise.

Juliette started to fidget. Being quiet just wasn't her thing.

'Would you like to see me do some cartwheels?' she asked smiling cutely at Dad. Before he could answer, she took up her position on the grass, like a real professional gymnast, and then did cartwheel after cartwheel.

When she finally stopped, she stood looking at us with her huge smile. She was gasping for breath but it still didn't stop her talking.

'I'm practising to be a gold...medal winner... When we go home to Montreal... I'm going to train on the performance...mat. My coach says... I might get good enough...to be in the Olympics... I know I'll have to practise for years.'

I realised then that I had been wrong the other day. Maybe Juliette will be in the Olympics one day. I remembered watching gymnasts at the Olympics on TV. They did do cartwheels as well as other things. And they certainly *did* get medals. They always seem to land exactly inside the performance mat. One toe outside and you lose points.

'Let's take Dad to see Moonlight,' I said.

We went down to the field. Together. There was a slight breeze moving through the leaves in the avenue of tall poplars. It was as if the trees were making their own kind of music.

I took some photos of Moonlight to help me later with my drawing for the Art Display.

'Abigay might get famous if her picture's in the hospital Art Display,' Juliette said to Dad. 'It's open to brothers and sisters and cousins of patients, you know. She's going to try drawing the foal. Gabriel said he doesn't know yet what he'll be entering.'

I wished she wouldn't talk about Gabriel as if she knew him. Correction – I wished she would just stop talking!

'Well, I don't know if I CAN draw ponies or foals well enough yet,' I said. 'Look Dad! He knows us. He's letting me stroke him.'

Moonlight's coat felt lovely and soft. – a warm sandy colour just like his mother. Beauty snorted as she moved her head up and down and swished her tail.

'See, Dad, you can tell she trusts us!'

Suddenly, Moonlight set off across the field on his spindly legs, then flicked his back legs up off the ground and then came racing back towards us.

'He's doing his exercises!' Juliette squealed. 'Clever boy!'

Dad got to know the Three Macs over a "quick lunch". Dave told Dad that long ago, he visited Kingston, Jamaica, when he belonged to a band.

'My parents went back there to retire,' Dad said. 'We try and see them as often as we can.'

When the conversation turned to the Open Farm, Grandpa shifted uncomfortably in his chair. Everyone was suddenly full of great ideas.

'We could have an area for kids to play in,' I said, 'like a playground with swings, a climbing frame and picnic benches?'

Good idea!' said Juliette in her overexcited way.

'And a zip wire too. Kids love them!'

Grandpa groaned. 'You just don't give up!' he said, ruffling my hair.

He was in such a good mood that I tried another idea.

'Maybe we can have something for the goats to climb on...like at the city farm?' I added but Grandpa was suddenly distracted. He kept looking at his watch.

'You'll have to be going soon if you want to see Gabriel this evening,' he said to Dad and me.

It was hard saying goodbye to the Three Macs.

'We'll miss you all, but I'm sure looking forward to going to Scotland,' Tammy said.

Of course, I felt sorry to say goodbye. Juliette can be a bit of a pain sometimes, but as Grandma would say, 'her heart is in the right place'. Mostly she's just really good fun. And I didn't know if we'd ever see each other again.

'Au revoir!' I said handing Juliette a sketch of Moonlight.

'I'll keep practising drawing and you keep practising cartwheels,' I said, laughing.

'Don't forget to ring me with updates,' Juliette said, giving me a big hug.

'I will,' I said.

It was a big farewell scene. I felt really quite sad. I didn't know it yet, but I would soon have something else to worry about. Something big.

Chapter 22

THE PHONE CALL

We drove slowly along the long bumpy drive before turning sharply onto the narrow country road. Dad wound the window down another couple of inches and picked up speed. For a while he sang a Jamaican folk song that I must have heard a thousand times. It still makes me laugh.

'Gosh! That was an interesting morning,' he said. 'I'm very impressed with you and Gabriel – a *proposal* no less… just like my undergraduate students!' His laugh boomed round the car.

I felt my cheeks go warm from the attention.

'I must say that this is the first time in ages that I've seen your grandfather in such a good mood,' Dad continued. 'And what about that Canadian family…what do they call themselves? The Three Macs. I enjoyed talking to them. If only we'd had more time. So, he's an artist as well as a musician. What talent!

'You can go to sleep when we hit the motorway, if you want,' Dad said, looking at his watch.

But as it turned out, this was the one journey where I definitely didn't sleep.

We had passed the first town after the farm when Dad's phone rang. I answered it for him. It was Mum.

'We're on our way,' I said cheerfully but Mum sounded anxious and flustered.

'I've been trying to contact your dad all morning,' she said. 'We need to talk urgently!'

'Tell her I'll stop as soon as I can,' said Dad. A few minutes later he pulled onto the grassy area where the woodland trail leads to the Downs.

He took the phone from me and wandered a little distance away.

'Sorry, love, I didn't realise my battery was dead,' I heard him say. 'I was charging it in the car just now.' As he paced up and down, it became clear something was wrong.

'When did this happen?' he said. 'And where is he now?'

I had a bad feeling in my stomach.

'OK then, we'll see you when we get there,' Dad said.

He sat down on the grass and waved me over. 'Sit for a minute, Abigay, and listen carefully. It's nothing to worry about, but they've gone ahead with Gabriel's operation unexpectedly today.'

I stared at Dad. He took my hand. His voice was calm, which helped to slow down my fast breathing.

'It's all been very quick but the upshot is that Gabriel's in the operating theatre right now! Just remember, he'll be fine and we shouldn't worry.'

I felt dreadful. I should have been there with him beforehand. I should be there for him when he wakes up. I felt like a terrible twin.

'So what are we waiting for, Dad?,' I shouted. 'Let's go!'

As soon as we got there we hurried across the almost-empty car park and entered the hospital through the revolving doors.

'He's bound to be drowsy after the anaesthetic,' Dad said, his voice echoing down the long corridor.

And he was right. Gabriel gave a little grin as we came into the ward. He didn't say much but I knew he was happy to see us – and I was *so* relieved to see him.

'I'm so glad you're here,' Mum said as she kissed us both. She looked tired.

'I – we – didn't know, Mum,' I gulped. 'As his twin, I should have known!'

All the bad things that *could have happened* flashed before my eyes. She gave me a big warm hug. I sighed deeply.

Nurse Josephine came bustling over to us.

'I'm glad you got here before I finish tonight,' she said. 'I'll be away for a few days' holiday. I'm handing over my special patient to Nurse Heather tomorrow.'

She gave me a high five and winked at Gabriel. 'You'd better behave yourself!' she said, her face creasing into a big smile.

When she was talking to Mum and Dad, Gabriel made his pretend important face. He likes to think he can raise his left eyebrow on its own. It never moves much but I haven't told *him* that.

'Cool!' I said. 'Have you been practising?'

He smiled weakly.

We didn't stay long at the hospital because Gabriel was drifting in and out of sleep. It had been such an emotional day and a BIG RELIEF to see Gabriel awake and smiling. I can't really explain it. I tried to write something beautiful about it in my notebook later to remember the day but, try as I might, I just couldn't find the right words.

But I'll never forget that day.

Chapter 23

SCHOOL

Mum says that twins sometimes get put in different classes at school. But not me and Gabriel. Even when we moved on to secondary school this year, we were put in the same tutor group. It meant all my friends and teachers knew about Gabriel and how he had often been in and out of hospital. Sometimes, when the pains and spasms were extra bad, he would have to stay in for up to ten days. In primary school, we did a class montage of the Amazon rainforest to put by his bed in the hospital. He really liked it – especially the parrot I had painted.

MAYBE, after this operation he won't have to go back to hospital anymore.

Back at school on Monday, Miss Davies the form tutor asked about Gabriel.

'He had the operation on his hip on Friday,' I said. 'He says he's practically bionic with all the metal pins holding his bones in place.'

Miss Davies smiled and some of the children laughed.

'Ugh! Gross!' sniggered Carl from the back of the class. Miss Davies threw him a frosty look.

'And the day after,' I carried on, 'they got him out of bed to sit on a chair. Soon he'll try a few steps with his crutches.'

'That's a good sign,' said Miss Davies. 'It's sensible to take things one step at a time.'

Miss Davies smiled her encouraging smile. She looked round at the class and repeated, 'One step at a time. That's a useful phrase to remember.' Miss Davies is big on useful phrases.

'Can we send him letters?' Miles asked. Miles is my brother's best friend – after me, of course!

Miss Davies smiled. 'Good idea, Miles,' she said. 'We shall send him the class news – perhaps we could tell all about the new geography and humanities project we'll be doing.

'This term, we'll be learning all about China,' she said, her eyes shining. 'I was there in the holidays, you know – it's a vast and fascinating country. We'll learn about the Great Wall and the many things the Chinese invented before the Western world did – like paper.'

'I want to do a project about Ibiza,' Johnny muttered. 'That's where *we* went last summer.'

Miss Davies didn't hear him, or she pretended not to.

The Activity Centre at the hospital always welcomes brothers and sisters. It's a big bright room with lots of windows. There are tables for arts and crafts and comfy chairs and loads of books for kids who want to sit quietly and read. If you're not well enough for standing-around activities, you can sit and play board games with the helpers.

When I came into the centre that Tuesday, I searched for Gabriel. I spotted him sitting in a wheelchair.

He was busy talking to a group of kids at one of the activity tables.

'Guess what?' he said when I sat down. 'The consultant said I'll be back at school in no time.'

I wanted to give him a big hug but of course I didn't, especially not in front of the others.

I noticed the bright-coloured sticks in the big new box with "Oil Pastel Crayons" printed across the lid.

I tried out the orange, brown, white and yellow shades.

'I've drawn Moonlight,' I said to Gabriel. 'Some of these colours could be just right for colouring it in. I can blend together a sandy colour for his back. Have you decided what to do for the display yet?'

'Maybe,' he answered. 'I'm still thinking about it.'

Why so mysterious and secretive, I thought.

'You can tell me,' I said. I tried not to sound disappointed but I really didn't like him keeping secrets from me.

It seemed like two whole days before Gabriel answered, 'Alright, since you're so desperate to know, I *have* done something for the Art Display. It isn't exactly drawing, it's lettering. Mr Hill, the art teacher, said lettering is an art form. It's finished and I've handed it in.'

'Can you at least tell me what it's about?' I asked, but Gabriel wouldn't say anything more.

'Well, I'm not keeping mine a secret,' I said.

I showed him the drawing of Moonlight. I had just finished colouring it in and I was pleased.

'I think it's ready to hand in,' I said.

'It's good!' Gabriel said.

I couldn't wait to see my drawing up at the Art Display and Gabriel's too, whatever this mysterious piece was.

Chapter 24

INVITATION

Gabriel was allowed home five days after his operation.

'Now all you have to do is to recover – no more going in and out of hospital,' I told him. 'It's great, isn't it?!'

'Yes. And I'll be having sessions in the hydrotherapy pool soon,' said Gabriel cheerfully. We were sitting at the kitchen table eating the chocolate cake I'd baked earlier. 'I bet you wish you could splash around in the lovely warm water too,' he added. 'And I'll have to go back to the hospital for physio exercises too.'

It was so great having Gabriel back home. He was just about getting the hang of his crutches again but, of course, he couldn't manage the stairs. He was still using the small downstairs room as a bedroom and sometimes we both slept there and chatted late into the night. There so much to talk about.

Grandma and Grandpa called every day to ask about Gabriel. Yesterday they said they had a meeting with the business advisor at the bank to discuss the Open Farm.

It all sounded very serious – business plans, budgets and 'projected earnings'. Gabriel sank back on his pillow.

'Let's hope Christopher King's dad isn't still skulking around trying to get Grandpa to sell. We don't want them finding out about our Open Farm idea! I don't trust them.'

'Me neither,' I said. 'Oh, by the way, Grandma has sent us some new photos of Moonlight. Look, here are two of him skittering around the field. He already looks much stronger and even more adorable.'

Later that week, the phone rang. As soon as I picked it up, someone started to speak really fast on the other end, her voice getting squeakier and squeakier.

'Hello Juliette,' I said.

'Tammy said I had to write a letter first before I rang you – it's part of a home school lesson. I sent it off yesterday afternoon. Did you get it? Did you have the Art Display yet? What did Gabriel do for it? Have you set a date to start the Open Farm?'

She was disappointed when I said no to all the questions.

'Don't worry,' I said. 'As soon as we have any news about the Open Farm, you'll be the first to know. And I'll take plenty of pictures of the Art Display on my phone – especially Gabriel's entry and mine.

'How was your trip to Scotland?' I asked quickly. I wanted to change the subject. It was bad enough that my twin *still* hadn't shared his secret with me and I couldn't bear her to talk about it.

'Scotland was *beautiful*!' she replied. 'Miles of silvery sands – BRILLIANT for gymnastics too and I love the rock pools!'

'Did Dave manage to find his roots?' I asked.

'Yes! We went to the tiny village where he was born. You know he had to walk miles just to get to school. There was no home-schooling in those days and the parents were way too busy looking after the animals and crops. He called on some neighbours from long ago and we had a fab time...'

I told Juliette that Gabriel had his operation and was back home. I finally managed to get her off the phone after what seemed like five and a half hours. Juliette's letter *did* arrive next morning.

Deer Abigay

Scotland is nice. We've reached the Hylands. We're going to visit a castl tody. We're goin on a ferry bote over to an iland called Mull. The Hylands don't have mountains as hy as in Canada. We are the winners, not you. So there!

Xxx Juliette

There was another letter in the post that morning in a fancy envelope.

'What can this be?' I said, showing it to Gabriel. Inside it was an even fancier invite on thick card.

Art Display
In aid of the Children's Ward
and Hospital Fund

'Oh. That's the invite to the preview on Saturday,' said Gabriel. 'My mate Rob's coming with his parents,' he said. 'You know we shared the same ward. You'll like him. He's a good laugh.'

I couldn't help feeling a tiny bit jealous but I was happy for Gabriel.

He went quiet then. I knew why. He and Rob had shared painful times as well as laughs. I know twins should share everything but it was still too early for us to talk about those days at the hospital.

Neither of us said anything for a bit.

Gabriel perked up. 'His mum goes around the world making nature documentaries. She's just come back from filming orangutans in Borneo. It'll be on TV soon.

'Anyway, about my entry, you'll get to see it. Not long now!' he added.

'You've been making such a BIG SECRET of it,' I groaned. 'It had better be good!'

Chapter 25

ART DISPLAY

I saw my picture straight away when we arrived at the official opening. It was just opposite the door as we came in. Mum and Dad loved it. I had drawn Moonlight lying down.

'Well done,' said Mum.

'Good job,' Dad said.

'Next time, I'll draw him standing on his spindly legs,' I said.

Gabriel dragged us to where Rob and his dad were staring at another picture. It was a large poster that stood out above everything else. I knew immediately whose work it was.

A beautiful willow tree framed a field of golden wheat ready for harvest with a few tiny red poppies along the side. But the most fantastic thing of all was Gabriel's calligraphy. The bold hand-drawn lettering across the wheat field spelt out the words:

Willowfield
WORKING FARM

OPEN
to the public

Schools & Families welcome

I stood and stared. I thought my picture was good but this was amazing. I never knew Gabriel could paint so well.

'Gabriel told me a lot about the farm,' Rob was saying to his dad. 'But he didn't say it was open to the public. Can we go there?'

'Well done, Gabriel,' said Dad. 'Very eye-catching indeed!'

By now a large group of people had gathered around the poster. Mum beamed with pride. I took a photo to show Juliette.

It was fun to walk around and see what everybody else had done for the Art Display. I knew the names of almost everyone.

We drifted over to the refreshments area where Rob and his parents joined us.

As people passed by, they stopped and shook hands with Rob's mum and made remarks about her films. It had been announced that someone famous would be attending the preview and everybody suddenly realised that that person was her – Gina Price.

Gabriel whispered to me, 'Rob told me his mum was famous but I didn't realise so many people would recognise her.'

He turned to Rob and carried on chattering. The grown-ups were all deep in conversation. That's when I had an idea. If an important person like Gina Price could help publicise the Children's Ward and Hospital Fund, then maybe she could do the same for Willowfield Farm.

I did something I'm not supposed to do. I interrupted the grown-ups.

'Mrs Price,' I said in a slightly shaky voice, 'if you liked Gabriel's poster then maybe you could come and film our Opening Day at Willowfield? It's all part of our big plan to save the farm. We want to open it to the public just like a city farm except this is a real working family farm in the countryside. You see, I got the inspiration when our foal Moonlight was born. He will be the main attraction.'

I suddenly realised that I was prattling on. Everyone had stopped talking and was looking at me. I felt dizzy.

Mum and Dad did not look pleased. Gabriel and Rob looked at me blankly. Gina Price was quiet and seemed to be thinking.

Help! I thought. Was that really pushy and rude?

Gina Price turned to me and smiled.

'Thank you, Abigay,' she said. 'What a lovely invitation. I have to say I can't make any promises right now but I will most certainly think about it.'

I knew grown-ups well enough to know when they're just being polite. Suddenly, I felt very hot, uncomfortable and extremely foolish.

Chapter 26

BACK TO NORMAL

Summer term rolled on.

Of course, Gabriel still wasn't back at school. Most days, he was busy with exercises and hydrotherapy sessions and sometimes he got impatient and frustrated.

Sometimes he wanted to hear about my day at school. If he didn't ask, I didn't say anything. He was interested in the class outing to the British Museum for the China project.

'How was it?' he asked.

'Good,' I said. 'Apart from when Kayla accidentally pulled a tassel off the red dragon. But we did get to see massive photographs of the Great Wall of China. That'll help with the model we're building in class.'

At night, when it was still and silent, Gabriel and I quietly plotted and planned and talked about Willowfield.

'I've had an idea for something the goats can climb on,' I said.

'Will it be like the railway embankment at the city farm?' Gabriel asked.

'No,' I said. 'It can't be down the hillside. It's all wooded there. It needs to be near the top field where people will see them and it'll be just as good. We can build a crazy mountain effect with big and small logs. and we can watch them leaping from one log to another.'

'And I've been doing some research online for the alpacas,' said Gabriel. 'Let's hope Grandpa doesn't go and change his mind about that!'

'Do you remember when we were small enough to sit on Rosie the donkey?' I asked.

Gabriel laughed. 'Yes! We can't do that anymore – we'd flatten her!'

'Remember the time Grandpa tried growing blackcurrants?' I said.

'Yeah! It was fun to watch that machine with the robot arms that stripped the fruit ever so gently,' said Gabriel.

'And what about all those people who came to help harvest the blackcurrants. Then we had those two really rainy summers during that time, didn't we?'

We both stopped talking. The farm had lost a lot of money then. Everyone was really worried. But then everything seemed to sort itself out.

'It was always great when we got new animals,' I said. 'Especially when Auntie Rachel bought Beauty – we were so excited. We got to see her every day, didn't we?'

'I've always liked our pot-bellied pigs,' said Gabriel.

'Do you remember when the sow had all those cute little piglets?'

'And what about that summer when we were first allowed to bottle-feed the orphan lambs. You had to be a bit strong the way they tugged so hard on the teat.'

'I can't wait to roam round the farm again,' said Gabriel. 'And to hang out down at the stream. I really miss that place.'

I'd noticed something interesting about Gabriel since all those hospital visits. He had changed. He had started reading even more books than me. Before, I was the one always borrowing books from the library.

'You're not now going to become a professor or something, are you?' I said. 'I thought you were dead set on going to agricultural college and being a farmer like me!'

'Don't be silly!' Gabriel laughed. 'Farmers are allowed to read too.'

We went together to the library and the children's park. He practised going around the playground with his crutches.

'This counts as my daily exercise. The physiotherapists will be pleased,' he said.

We sat down on the big rock and read our library books. We talked. Sometimes we just sat in silence. Life felt good.

Chapter 27

MAKING PLANS

I was woken from a deep sleep by a loud, triumphant crowing.

What on earth? I thought as I rolled over and tried to block the noise out by covering my ears. Then I remembered. It was Half Term. I was back at Willowfield – once again in this lovely little bedroom with the dark wooden beams and the flowery curtains. And out there was the cockerel!

I told myself he was welcoming me back but of course he makes the same triumphant call every morning, whether or not I'm there. After a couple of days, my brain knows instinctively to ignore it so I can sleep on a bit.

I thought of Gabriel back home. He'll be hearing the gentle sound of the traffic and, if he's lucky, maybe a robin or a blackbird singing.

Such a lot had happened since I last slept in that little room. I remembered that terrible time when Grandma and Grandpa were arguing. Then the rush back to London to see Gabriel after his operation.

Gabriel had so wanted to be here for the half-term but he still wasn't ready to sit in the car for such a long journey. And in the end, he couldn't make it back to school either before half-term. He was still limping. I thought the operation would sort that out. He was working hard on fixing it with the exercises. At least he had a project to keep him busy.

'The art project leader showed me how to set up a website,' he'd said. 'I'll work on it while you're there and you can send me photos of Moonlight, Rosie, the pigs, the hens, the farm cats and all the rest. I'll do the layout.'

When I arrived at the farm the evening before, Grandpa showed me the business plan and the budget for the Open Farm. I couldn't help remembering his outburst at that very same table – it couldn't have been more different now.

This time he explained everything to me carefully, showed me how the figures added up and how much we needed to earn to make the whole thing work.

He talked to me in a grown-up way.

I told him about Gabriel's website.

'We'll share ideas and decide together what to put on it, then he'll do the rest,' I'd said.

'I'm sure you'll do a good job between you,' Grandma had said. 'The plan is to open the farm to the public next Easter – provided we get the go-ahead from the bank.'

I was wondering why they would wait such a long time, when I was roused from my thoughts by a loud ringtone. I reached out to grab my phone from the bedside table and knocked it on the floor. A couple of seconds later I was scrambling under the bed trying to find it.

'Ouch!' I cried as I bumped my head on the bottom of the bed frame.

'Abigay!' screamed a familiar voice, when I finally found the phone. 'Look out your window!'

I crawled out from under the bed and limped to the window.

'I can't see anything,' I said rubbing my head.

Then slowly, I saw the unmistakable mauve and white van creep slowly over the hill.

'CAN YOU SEE US NOW?' screamed Juliette.

'Yes!' I said. 'I thought you were still in Scotland.'

'Not any longer!' squealed Juliette.

I ran to tell Grandma. 'The Three Macs have just driven into the farm,' I panted. 'Did you know anything about this?'

Grandma was clearly trying not to smile. 'When I was your age, I used to love surprises.

'Actually, it was Tammy Mac who contacted me,' she laughed. 'She said Juliette would love to come back to the farm now that you're here. And besides, Dave wants to carve some wooden animals to create a sculpture trail for the farm. Children will love trying to find them.'

'What, like a treasure trail?' I asked. I liked the sound of that.

The scrunching of tyres echoed around the yard. The Three Macs had arrived. I rushed out to say hello.

'Good to see you!' said Dave, jumping down from the driver's seat.

I'd forgotten how strong his accent was and how big he looked.

'Look, man!' he said. 'No ponytail.'

I thought he meant Juliette, except that she usually wore her hair in bunches, but he pointed to his own head and did a twirl. He looked so different with short hair.

Juliette tumbled out of the back of the van, followed by Tammy.

She was still screaming. 'This is the best surprise visit I've *ever* done! Did we surprise you?'

She grabbed my hand.

'Let's go and see Moonlight and Beauty. Come on! Let's go!'

We hurried down the hill and found them in the shelter at the far side of the field. They often stand there when it's hot.

Moonlight came over to us and let us stroke his nose. We told him how beautiful he was. It was like he could understand.

Early in the evening, I remembered that Gabriel had asked me to send him a letter with all the farm news when I arrived, so I did.

Willowfield Farm.
Saturday

Hi Gabriel

Next time I come to the farm you'll be coming too — hooray!

It's evening but it's not dark. I'm sitting on the wooden bench by the kitchen, drawing the farm cats. Grandma said there's no wild cats in England. She likes to call our farm cats independent cats because they catch their own food.

Question:
What happened to the cat who swallowed
a ball of wool?

Answer:
She had mittens.

Tomorrow we're going to the Village Fete. And guess what? The Three Macs have come back to camp here for a few days. We're taking Juliette with us to the fete. Grandma's not too pleased about it, but Tammy will be busy doing a painting of the farm and Dave's got lots of planning to do for the sculpture trail. He's going to be carving a hare out of an old tree stump. He usually charges a lot for his sculptures but he wants to do all these for free!!!

Don't forget to do your exercises.

Bye for now.
Abigay

Ps How's the website going?

As I was going to bed that night, Grandma said, 'Tomorrow, at the fete, please don't tell people about our plan for the Open Farm. And we must tell Juliette not to say anything as well. For now, it's got to be top secret. We don't want anyone else stealing our idea now, do we?'

Chapter 28

VILLAGE FETE

Taking Juliette round the stalls at the Village Fete was better than I thought – at first anyway. Every year it's held in the big field behind the church. Most of the field is surrounded by hedgerows and there's a row of tall trees at the far end.

We came in through the church hall where the teas were being served. Everything looked light and bright from the freshly painted walls to the crisp, posh tablecloths. From there, we followed the decorations, flags and bunting down to the entrance to the field.

This is where Gabriel and I usually stand to take it all in. Except this time, it was Juliette beside me who looked wide-eyed at everything laid out in front of us.

On one side there was the white elephant stall, followed by the tombola, book stall, prize vegetable stand, face-painting table, art and craft displays and my favourite of all – the big CAKE tent! On the opposite side of the field the games and competitions had already started – these would continue throughout the day.

'I'm so mega-excited!' said Juliette as she skipped along. 'England is so cute!' she squealed.

People smiled at her shiny face and any time she found a clear patch of grass she started doing cartwheels and walking on her hands.

'Who's your little friend?' they asked. The more impressed they were at her skills, the more she showed off. That is, until the field started to fill up so much, there was no space left for gymnastics.

We had pocket money to spend, so we had a go at the stall where you smash as much china as possible by throwing a wooden ball. There were no prizes for the winners but I wouldn't have got one anyway – I hardly hit any plates. Juliette had more luck but the sound of the breaking china made her laugh so much she couldn't throw straight anymore.

We tried the welly wanging stall – everything seemed to be about throwing this year. I imagined my boot would soar through the air and land far away but, actually, it was heavy and awkward to throw and didn't go far at all. Still it was fun. Juliette didn't do well either. She wouldn't talk about it – she likes to WIN.

She did cheer up when we noticed the tug of war starting up – it was the Young Farmers of Bromwell v neighbouring Penfold. There was lots of loud grunting and groaning as the piece of red cloth tied to the middle of the rope went back and forth over the white line in the dry ground. The red-faced young farmers looked fit to burst as each side dug in their heels and heaved.

In the end, the locals – Bromwell Young Farmers – won. They hauled the rope one last time and Penfold collapsed in a heavy heap of sweaty bodies to the sound of cheers and jeers and laughter.

We had just bought a cornet with a big flake and a bright pink ice lolly from the ice cream van when things suddenly started to go wrong.

I happened to glance over to the entrance to the field.

'Oh no!' I groaned. 'Not Christopher King!'

Christopher walked straight over to us with a nasty look on his face.

'Who's SHE?' he asked rudely, pointing his grubby finger at Juliette.

'Why don't you ask her yourself?' I said. 'She does speak, you know!'

Before Christopher had a chance to answer, Juliette came right up to him and proclaimed in a loud voice, 'I'm Juliette. I'm from Canada. I'm nearly eight.'

Christopher wasn't impressed. He just stared blankly.

'Staring at people is rude,' said Juliette. 'Don't you know that?'

I had to laugh. Christopher then looked straight at me.

'You think you're so high and mighty, living in the big city. You won't be so high and mighty when your *ancient* grandad has to sell his farm. My dad will buy it and that includes the stream.'

I didn't notice Juliette pushing forward until it was too late. She gave Christopher a swift kick in the shin.

'Why are you so nasty?' she screamed. 'Abigay's grandpa isn't going to sell his farm and her family are ALWAYS going to own it. *And* they are going to open it to the public. People will be paying to come in and learn

about working farms today. So there!'

Oh NO! I thought. This is bad. For a moment Christopher looked confused. He seemed to be fishing for ideas.

'Well, you know what?' he suddenly snarled. 'My dad's going to open our farm *too* and it's going to be *way* better than your poxy Open Farm. We've even got a name for it already.'

He thought for a second, then puffed out his chest and announced – 'The West Country Experience!'

I looked round and searched for Grandma or Grandpa. This was really bad, I thought. I started to pull Juliette away.

'Leave him,' I said. 'He's not worth it! He's just a liar. He's made that up!'

That's when Christopher began making a weird wailing sound like a pig in pain, pretending his leg was badly hurt. How low can you sink? I thought.

'He wants to get us in trouble,' I said to Juliette. 'But nobody can hear him over the loud music.'

We walked away and found a bench to sit on.

That's when Juliette did something I wasn't expecting at all. She started to cry, quietly at first, then really noisily.

'I'm not supposed to kick people,' she said in between sobs. 'Abigay, please don't tell Tammy and Dave. Promise?'

A lady with silver hair passed in front of us. She looked concerned.

'Are you two OK? You look a bit bothered. Is there anything I can do to help?'

The lady was so kind, we couldn't help telling her what had happened – including the bit about the Open Farm.

Another mistake!

Grandma suddenly appeared in front of us.

'Are these girls with you?' said the lady. 'They seem a little upset.'

Grandma and the lady talked for a while. Then, we made our way to the car park.

'Grandma! It was so unfair!' I said as we climbed into the old Landrover.

'Christopher King was being horrible.' I nearly choked on the words but I had to tell her everything – that is, everything except the bit where Juliette kicked Christopher.

'Oh dear!' said Grandma. 'We're going to have to discuss this.'

Before we left the village, we passed by Auntie Rachel's house.

'Goodness! The West Country Experience no less,' said Auntie Rachel. She thought for a bit. 'They'd need permission for something on that scale, wouldn't they? It could all be made up. I haven't heard any mention of it in the parish council or anywhere else, have you, mother?' She turned to Grandma who shook her head.

For the first time in history, Juliette said nothing.

'Not to worry, Abigay,' said Auntie Rachel, putting her arm around my shoulders and ruffling Juliette's hair. 'Our Open Farm will be up and running well before they get such a thing going.'

'But the whole village is going to know soon,' said Grandma. 'If Grandpa agrees, maybe we need to bring the start date forward – just to be on the safe side.'

Suddenly, the clouds began to lift; that was exactly what I wanted to hear.

Chapter 29

ART TRAIL

'Abigay Miller here,' I said to Gabriel. 'Official photographer of the Willowfield Open Farm project.'

Every evening I bombarded Gabriel with photos.

'That West Country Experience thing is never going to happen,' he kept saying but I knew he had a niggling doubt. He was working extra hard on the website.

I took some good pictures of Grandpa using the milking machine and Grandma milking a cow the old-fashioned way.

I also took some of the fields, the farmhouse, Grandpa driving the tractor, and a spinning wheel that the family used to use in the old days. I made sure to include some close-ups of chicks, ducks and piglets for the younger children. My favourite photo of all was of Auntie Rachel brushing Beauty with Moonlight looking on.

Naturally, Juliette shadowed me everywhere and even took a few blurry photos of the hens pecking in the farmyard.

Now we were climbing over the gate into the field where Rosie the donkey was standing by the far hedge.

'Of course the website has got to show the oldest animal on the farm,' I explained to Juliette.

At first, Rosie behaved like a camera-shy celebrity but with a bit of coaxing and a few friendly pats, I got the photos I needed.

'Come on, let's go,' said Juliette racing back towards the gate. 'Let's photograph the barn next.' Juliette always seemed to be in a rush.

Inside the now clean and tidy barn we photographed my ring of hay bales still laid out like a golden symbol of hope, before we headed out of the side door and around by the big solid lean-to. This is where Grandpa stored the massive sections of tree trunk from the trees that had fallen during the big storm two winters ago.

We were stopped in our tracks by the sight of Dave, Tammy and my grandparents standing by the lean-to. Dave was staring mysteriously at the giant chunks of wood while Grandma, Grandpa and Tammy watched in silence.

'What are you all looking at?' shouted Juliette.

Nobody moved.

'Tell me!' she shrieked.

Dave held his hand up for silence, rubbed his chin and continued to look thoughtful.

'He's choosing the blocks of wood for the sculpture trail,' Grandma said in hushed tones.

Dave climbed over the large shapes and checked them out from different angles. Then he stood still again with a glazed expression on his face. Finally, after what seemed like forever, he reached out his hand and took the paintbrush dripping with white paint from Grandpa. He climbed over the huge tree stumps and painted a big fat X on ten of them.

Grandpa had his ancient tractor ready and waiting, fitted with the forklift attachment. By early afternoon, he had moved the ten tree trunk sections to a clearing at the edge of the wood and placed them standing in a wide circle.

'Just like Stonehenge,' said Juliette, clapping her hands gleefully.

Tammy used the white paint to mark out a large circle in the ground around the tree trunks.

'Now,' said Dave, 'these are the rules. While work is going on here, no one must enter the white circle. At other times you may do so only if I'm here.'

We all agreed. He gave an extra-long look at Juliette who nodded like crazy.

We watched as chisels of all shapes and sizes and wooden hammers – mallets they're called – were brought in to the circle. And then – most surprising of all – Grandpa's chainsaw from the barn!

'I bet you've never seen a sculptor sculpt with a chainsaw before, Abigay?' said Dave.

I shook my head in disbelief.

'Some people do all the work by chainsaw but I like to use hand tools for the delicate bits,' he added.

'And these are the most important things of all,' he said, showing us a pair of goggles and a pair of ear defenders. 'This baby's going to make a whole heap of noise.

'Ladies and gentleman,' Dave then proclaimed, 'let the carving commence!'

He wasn't joking about the noise either. As he cut into the wood, the whining and buzzing was deafening for us, even from where we were standing. Clouds of sawdust swirled up around him and the smell of dry wood was everywhere. I could see Juliette – mouth wide open, eyes scrunched closed and hands over her ears – but for once there was something louder drowning out her screams.

As the days passed, a thick carpet of woodchips and sawdust formed inside Dave's circle.

He was working on all ten blocks of wood at the same time and all day long we could hear the whine of the chainsaw and thud, thud, thud of the mallets hitting the chisels.

Slowly we could see the animals starting to emerge from the blocks of wood. We had so much fun trying to guess what they were going to be. The first one we recognised was the giant hedgehog. Next we guessed the hare. The long ears were a giveaway of course but we'd figured it out long before, from its big feet.

'I know you love squirrels,' Dave said, 'and the clever way they jump from branch to branch! I'm going to make two squirrels chasing each other.'

He selected two pieces of wood and kept moving them around.

'I like to picture the shapes in my head long before I start to carve the wood,' he said.

While Dave was busy working, Tammy walked around, deep in thought.

'I want to paint a really large view of the farm, in acrylics,' she said to Grandma. 'You can hang it in the café if you like, or use it on the website – it's up to you. It will be my gift to the Open Farm for all your kindnesses.'

She finally decided to take up position on the ridge.

'This way I can include part of the wood,' she said, 'as well as the nearest field, the farmhouse and the barns. I'm going to try and capture the light at the golden hour just before sunset – I can't believe how different the light is here from Canada.'

I started drawing the cartoons for the display boards. I showed Tammy a big googly germ ready to pounce on children who did not wash their hands. Tammy laughed when she saw it.

'You're not just a good artist and photographer, you're a cartoonist too! Is there no end to your talents?'

When Grandma and Grandpa weren't doing the farm chores or making countless trips back and forth to Dave and Tammy with cups of tea, they were pouring over catalogues of log cabins and picnic tables.

And all of the time we hoped and hoped that the loan from the bank would finally be approved and our dream could finally become a reality.

Chapter 30

UPS AND DOWNS

Miss Davies likes to say 'when one door closes, another one opens', but maybe sometimes it should be the other way around. Sometimes a door opens only to have another slam with a big loud bang.

I joined Mum and Gabriel who were looking at the little screen of Grandma's phone.

'Hello Grandma! It's me.'

I was back in London, getting ready for school.

Grandma waved. 'Hello Abigay. Good. I'm glad you're there as well. I've got something amazing to show you all.'

Grandma has never really worked out how to use her phone. The picture waved about before we got a clear shot of Grandma's ear, then shots of empty sky, then the ground. Two black and white speckled hens strolled into view and one fat brown one moved quickly out of the way of Grandma's feet. The farm cats wandered slowly into the picture – as usual, not bothered with anybody or anything.

'Look up there!' said Grandma.

She pointed the phone up to the sky again and then we saw Grandpa's elbow and, finally, Grandpa himself. He was grinning into the phone camera from the top of a ladder.

'Just look at this wonderful sight!' said Grandma. 'I've been nagging him to fix that roof for months.'

'Hello there!' said Grandpa. 'Just doing a bit of mending. Got to make the whole place shipshape to meet the great British public. Has Grandma told you the news yet?'

I looked at Gabriel, then at Mum. Mum looked at me. Her eyebrows shot up and her eyes opened wide.

'Are you telling me what I think you're telling me?'

'Did the bank say YES?' I burst out.

Grandma's smile told us everything we needed to know.

'I CAN'T BELIEVE IT!'

Mum and I and Gabriel hugged each other and blew kisses at the phone.

'Now we can *really* start planning!' said Grandma. 'As soon as we got the news, Grandpa sprung up the ladder like a two-year-old.'

'What a wonderful day!' Mum laughed.

Everything was right with the world.

I looked in my diary to see how many weeks there were before the Open Farm began. I counted nine.

Life was busy at school too and so much better now that Gabriel was there.

Miss Davies gave Gabriel a warm welcome when he returned. 'Go easy on him, class,' she said. 'And don't wear him out!'

Despite Miss Davies' words, people were nosy, crowding around and asking strange questions. Gabriel liked the fuss at first but he soon got tired of all the attention. Things settled down and as time went on, he became just one of the class again.

We talked a lot with Grandma and Grandpa too. It seemed like all our ideas were becoming reality and so much more too. We had video calls and could see all the new developments. The wooden cabin for the tearoom had now been bought and put up in super-fast time. The first thing you saw when you entered was Tammy's amazing painting covering the whole of the back wall. A small shop section was planned. It was going to have pocket money toys for children to buy as souvenirs.

'I'm building a viewing platform above the milking parlour,' Grandpa said. 'People will be able to look down and see the cows and the milking machines.'

And there was the children's play area. Grandpa was already making the slide and picnic benches. Everything was falling into place.

But then one day at school, I looked across the classroom at Gabriel and got a shock. He didn't look great at all. At break time Miss Davies felt his forehead.
'You seem a little feverish,' she said. 'Let's get you home, just to be on the safe side.'

I felt a cold chill run through my body.

Mum came as soon as the school secretary rang. I hurried home at the end of the school day.

'Gabriel is in bed,' she said. 'The light is hurting his eyes so I've drawn the curtains. You can pop in for a moment but don't talk to him. What he needs now is plenty of sips of water and a good sleep. That should do the trick.' She let out a deep sigh. 'At least I hope so,' she said.

What I remember next is the sound of the dreadful coughing through the night. When the doctor came in the next morning, Gabriel was ordered straight to hospital where he could be watched carefully. He was put in a side room in the ward next to his old one.

After that, the days felt very long. Gabriel was having tests and I wasn't allowed to visit.

On Wednesday, Mum said, 'We think it would be good for you to go and stay on the farm, Abigay, as soon as school finishes on Friday.'

'But I want to be here when Gabriel comes home,' I said.

'We don't know how long that will be, love,' Dad said. 'And anyway,' he added, 'when he's better we'll all be joining you there.'

'But nobody's telling me what's wrong with him, so how do you know he'll be getting better or WHEN that will happen...? And another thing,' I said, 'everybody said the operation would make him better, so he could walk without pain. NOW HE'S EVEN TOO ILL TO WALK! So who are we supposed to believe?'

'Abigay,' said Mum, wrapping me in a hug, 'you *know* his hip is healing. Look how well he can walk now. This is something quite different and we don't have all the answers yet. The test results will be back any day and we'll let you know as soon as we find out anything.'

In the end, it was decided. It was the first time I wasn't happy to go to Willowfield Farm and there wasn't a thing I could do about it.

Things couldn't possibly get any worse! But as Miss Davies always says, 'it never rains but it pours' – sometimes I hate Miss Davies' sayings.

Chapter 31

THE ACCIDENT

I felt Grandpa's footsteps thudding on the ground before I saw him. He was running towards me where I stood by the edge of the field.

'What's h-happened?' he wheezed.

I grabbed his hand. 'Come! ...It's Moonlight!' I gasped trembling at how much blood there was. But that wasn't the worst of it. Moonlight's front leg was sticking out at a weird angle. I was so afraid it might be broken.

Grandpa knelt down and stroked the little foal. He looked at the leg and felt it, trying to avoid the wound.

'It's stopped bleeding but we need to ring Theresa the vet straight away.' He reached into his pocket for his mobile.

'Will he be alright Grandpa?' I asked. 'The vet will be able to help, won't she? Say he'll be alright.' My mouth felt as if it was filling up with cotton wool. My throat hurt and I could hardly speak. I nearly choked on the words. 'Will he die?'

Grandpa stood up. 'Not if we can help it, Abigay!' he said. 'You need to keep strong! They can work wonders nowadays.' Grandpa was punching the numbers into his phone.

'Grandpa, I think it was my fault,' I managed to say. I was holding back the tears. 'I called Moonlight over to the fence and then there was a dreadful noise that frightened him. He'd have been alright if he stayed at the other side of the field.'

Grandpa bent down again to comfort Moonlight, then he looked up at me. 'No it's not your fault, Abigay. If it's anybody's fault, it's mine. I did a lazy job on that fence. I should have removed that barbed wire.'

Before I could say anything, somebody called out loudly.

'Helloooo!'

Theresa the vet had driven her car right down the slope. She jumped out and went straight to Moonlight.

'That cut looks nasty and jagged. Let's clean it straight away. He's going to need a tetanus shot and then I want to get him to the horse hospital to have that leg looked at properly. It might just be a torn tendon but it's best to be sure.'

I stared at her. I thought everything would be fine once she arrived but now the serious look on her face gave me the shivers. *Hospital*!

'Can't you treat him here?' I asked.

But Theresa didn't seem to hear me. She looked around. 'Something must have scared him. Do you know what happened? Were either of you here at the time?'

My heart was beating fast.

'It was when Mr King's old-fashioned plane flew overhead,' I said. I saw Grandpa frowning at the mention of Mr King and his plane.

'It was flying low and the engine was spluttering. Suddenly, there was a *really* loud BANG! It made me jump! I watched as the plane circled over the hill to the landing strip.

'When I turned around, I saw that it had spooked Moonlight too. He was lying on the ground – on MY side of the fence. I don't even know how it was possible. He was whinnying. Beauty came to see what was wrong. And that's when I saw his leg.'

'Not good!' Theresa said. 'Not good!' She stood up and rang the surgery.

'We need a horse ambulance to take an injured foal to the hospital.'

She glanced over at us and put her thumb up. 'They're coming as soon as they can!' she said.

'But won't Moonlight be frightened being all alone?' I asked.

'Yes. You're right,' said Theresa. 'Sorry I should have explained. I'm going to ask them to take Beauty along too. Before they arrive, let's get that wound cleaned again and a temporary bandage put on. Come over and help me.'

I stroked Moonlight and talked to him in a soothing voice. He calmed down and was still. At least he wasn't going to be sent all alone to the hospital.

After that, we waited. Grandma wandered down to talk to Theresa for a while, then everyone went quiet.

It seemed like AGES before we heard the sound of the engine and the rattling of the trailer. The rescuers reached us and the horsebox swept round in a big circle before they stopped. They examined the pony carefully and helped Moonlight into a standing position. It was hard. They coaxed Beauty into the horsebox first and that encouraged Moonlight to follow.

We watched in silence while the horsebox disappeared from sight, taking them both away. Theresa followed and we were left staring at the empty field. Grandma took my hand as we walked back slowly to the farm. I kept thinking to myself, everything everywhere is going wrong. First Gabriel and now Moonlight. Both in hospital

Chapter 32

WAITING AND HOPING

I stared out of the window onto the farmyard. All was quiet. The hens were inside their hut, safe from the fox. The jackdaws were busy flying around the barn roof. The farm cats were nowhere to be seen. In the distance, I could see the line of poplar trees that Grandpa had planted when he was a very young man – fifty he said there were. They stood out now as tall silhouettes on the horizon. My heart was full of love for the farm but my head was full of worries.

I remembered what Grandpa had said – his exact words: 'When you've got hope, all sorts of things are possible.'

And I did try to have hope but it wasn't easy. With all that had happened, our well-thought-out plans had slowed to a standstill. We were still waiting to hear the results of Gabriel's tests. And Moonlight, our star attraction, was still in hospital. In the end, I must have gone back to sleep because I remember waking up with a fluttery, butterfly feeling still in my stomach.

The morning dragged on. I didn't feel like doing much. Most of the time, I just sat on the swing. I heard a car drive up but didn't bother to go and see who it was. Fifteen minutes later, Auntie Rachel appeared from around the side of the house and strolled over to where I sat.

'Well, I hope that little fellow doesn't give me any more shocks like that,' she said. She bent down and picked up a white and bluish feather from the ground and stroked the back of her hand slowly with it.

'I've just spoken to Theresa,' she said. 'The leg's not broken – it's mainly damage to the tendon. As soon as it starts to heal, they can both be brought back home again. Grandpa says we'll put them in the field behind the house. That way we can all keep an eye on him.' She looked at me.

'Cheer up, Abigay,' she said. 'I know you're worried about Gabriel too but you know he will surprise us all and pull through. Life's full of surprises, you know – we've had a few bad ones, but I think we're now due a few good ones!

Later, as I wandered aimlessly around the farmyard, the postwoman arrived. She jumped out of the van and crunched across the gravel with a bundle of envelopes.

'Mainly bills I'm afraid,' she chirped pointing to a brown envelope. 'This one is for diesel fuel. And that one looks like your fertiliser bill.

'Apart from that, just the one postcard from the Three Macs in Cornwall,' she continued, handing me the card. 'Sounds like Tammy is in her element painting rocky coves and seascapes. Oh! And Juliette says hello. They do get around that family, don't they?'

It wasn't for nothing they called the postwoman the eyes and ears of the village.

Grandma emerged from the farmhouse and took the post from me.

'Put the kettle on, Deborah,' said the postwoman. 'I'm gasping for a drink.' She followed us into the kitchen. 'Can't stop too long, mind – no rest for the wicked, as they say.'

Grandma put the card up on the shelf in the dresser for all to see. It reminded me that I still hadn't checked out Dave's sculpture trail. I wanted to see it for the first time with Gabriel, but I really needed cheering up today and I knew Gabriel would understand.

I left Grandma and the postwoman nattering in the kitchen and made my way back outside again.

I was curious to see what Dave had made. I'll pretend I'm a visitor to the farm, I thought.

At the edge of the wood, I stood and looked down the steep grassy bank to the village below. I turned towards the painted wooden sign with the carved words "Sculpture Trail" before stepping from the bright, hot sun into the cool, dappled shade. I let my eyes get used to the gloom then headed down the woodland path.

Some of the sculptures were easy to spot, coming into view as you turned a bend in the trail. Others were cleverly hidden in the landscape, like the badger peering out from its underground home, anxiously watching its tiny cub. Most farmers consider them a nuisance but Dave wanted to represent all the animals in the area. 'Well, I suppose a wooden one can't do much harm,' Grandpa had chuckled.

Further on, a fox with an enormous bushy tail crouched in the undergrowth ready to spring forward and sprint along ahead of me. With each additional animal, I gasped in amazement. A giant frog sat on a huge wooden lily pad and observed me moodily as I passed, two squirrels chased across a pile of fallen logs, and an upright hare stood inquisitively in the tall grass.

At the end of the trail was a beautiful deer – you could just about see it behind a small tree. I stood and stared. It was a doe. No antlers but it stood tall – as tall as me – and it was so graceful. It felt so real, I was almost afraid to move, afraid I would startle it and send it darting deep into the woods.

As lovely as the sculpture trail was – and it was so much better than I could ever have imagined – what I really missed was having Gabriel to talk to about it. All I could hear was a small rustling of a breeze among leaves and the sound of my footsteps on the path. I walked slowly, out of the wood.

Everything around me felt empty. The silent barn with its ring of hay bales. The teahouse I had passed on the way, still, empty and waiting, the landscape across the back wall a past moment in time created by a person now far away.

From where I was standing, I could see the post van in the distance disappearing off over the hill, followed by Auntie Rachel's little blue car. It seemed like everyone had gone away – the Three Macs, Gabriel, Moonlight and Beauty, Auntie Rachel, even Gladys the nosy postwoman. Back at the farmhouse, I half expected Grandpa and Grandma to have gone too.

Chapter 33

TWINS

There was a secret place above the milking parlour. Gabriel and I had discovered it on another lazy day, a summer long ago. Even though we knew it wasn't allowed, we climbed the hidden ladder around the back. We were little and it always gave us a thrill doing something we knew we shouldn't.

At the top there was a tiny door. We squeezed ourselves into the small wooden space. We crouched inside and held our breaths. The farm sounds reached us from all around but inside it felt quiet and safe as if nothing could touch us. We peeped through the big cracks between the dark, uneven floorboards and soon saw Grandpa arrive. We watched as he went about milking the cows. We were convinced he had no idea that two pairs of eyes were spying on him from the secret hiding place above.

Now the little door seemed so much smaller. I just managed to squeeze inside. It felt like the tiny house in *Alice in Wonderland*. I struggled to move. I had outgrown our secret place.

So much had changed over the years. As I crouched there, I thought about before, when we worried about silly things like cuts and bruises. Now with Gabriel's illness, and the farm, we had big things to worry about. Things that couldn't be fixed with a sticking plaster.

If our plans worked, then the secret place would soon be gone to make way for the visitors' platform. Where we once peeped down like spies through the cracks in the floor, strangers would look down through a viewing window. We wouldn't be just giving up our secret place though; the whole of Willowfield would be shared and on show. That's what Gabriel and I had pushed for! But the success of our plans rested on the big IF.

I heard my Auntie's voice calling, faint and distant. It was time to leave my hiding place one last time and return to reality.

I wandered back by the pond and passed beneath the shade of the biggest willow tree. Nothing was stirring on the surface of the water or in the air – not even a dragonfly.

The vet said that the horse ambulance would be arriving at 1.00pm. Long after that, we were all still waiting on the garden bench outside the kitchen. Auntie Rachel said we were a proper reception committee.

At long last, we heard the sound of the heavy vehicle coming up the drive. We jumped up. It seemed to take forever for the horsebox to be opened up and for the ramp to come down. Finally, when the ponies emerged, Beauty came first, followed by Moonlight. I noticed he was still limping badly.

'Don't worry,' said Grandma when she saw my face. 'That's to be expected.'

We led Beauty into the big double stable but left it open so she was free to go into the field. In about ten seconds, she was out in the open again.

'Welcome back my lovely Beauty,' I called as I went into the small stable.

My eyes adjusted to the dark inside. I was sure Auntie Rachel had come in here with Moonlight – but where was she? I peered into the silent gloom, waiting for my eyes to adjust a bit more. The world seemed to stand still. Then a loud voice came from directly behind me.

'I heard you might be looking for help with a foal!'

Startled, I nearly jumped out of my skin. I turned. For a moment, I stood frozen to the spot and stared. Large as life, standing there, was Gabriel!

Then to my huge shame, I did something *super* embarrassing. I started to cry – not a gentle weeping but a full on, six-year-old-style blubbering. I didn't know whether I was crying with happiness or crying for everything that had happened before, everything I had held inside. Maybe it was a bit of both. All I knew was the floodgates had opened and there wasn't a thing I could do about it.

A thousand thoughts swirled around in my brain – Moonlight's birth in the silvery moonlight, the time capsule, Grandpa getting angry, Dave's sculpture trail, Juliette's constant chattering, days spent at the hospital and time spent on my own, Gabriel's operation, the art competition, Christopher's taunting at the Village Fete, and for some strange reason the Great Wall of China was bobbing around in the muddled-up mix.

'And here's me thinking you'd be pleased to see me,' said Gabriel giving me a playful punch on the arm.

Of course, that made me splutter and laugh. Suddenly, we were both laughing and jumping up and down gleefully – well, I jumped up and down. Gabriel just did his best to keep his balance.

'But you're not even supposed to be here,' I said, wiping my face. 'You're supposed to be sick!'

'Well excuse me for not being sick anymore,' said Gabriel. 'Oh, and it was a chest infection by the way – thanks for asking. The doctors decided I didn't have the superbug after all. They prescribed a nice farm holiday and what better farm than Willowfield?'

'But why didn't you tell me?!' I said giving him a push, then remembering and grabbing him to stop him falling over.

'Oops, sorry,' I said. 'So why didn't you tell me?'

'What and spoil the surprise!' said Gabriel grinning like an idiot. 'No way!'

'Well, now you're finally here, there's someone special you should meet.'

I dragged Gabriel by the wrist and started leading him to the back of the stable.

'Oh and by the way, don't you dare tell anyone I cried,' I warned him.

I looked at Gabriel's face; it was so different from the last time I saw him. Before, he could hardly lift his eyelids and now his eyes shone with mischief.

'Don't worry,' he said. 'Your secret's safe with me. Well, for now anyway.'

*

Moonlight looked so tiny at the back of the stable. I made encouraging noises and he came limping towards me. I stroked him and patted him gently.

'You are my perfect little star!' I said in his wonderfully soft ear. 'You'll be nice and safe here. This new field has a good high fence. The vet has told that crazy show-off farmer not to fly over our land and frighten you ever again!'

Maybe it was me going all gooey over Moonlight that did it, or the idea of the vet imposing a no-fly zone over Willowfield, but pretty soon Gabriel was cracking up again. Of course that set me off. There we were, twins laughing together until our chests hurt and our legs felt wobbly.

'Come,' I said, moving Gabriel over. 'Moonlight needs to get to know you.'

Gabriel peered at the little foal. 'He's even more cute than I thought,' he said. 'He'll easily be the star of the Open Farm.'

He stroked and patted Moonlight gently.

'It's almost like he knows you,' I whispered.

Our little star began to follow us when we eventually left. We shut the half door behind us. He was so tiny that he could hardly see over it.

Out in the bright sunlight our entire family was waiting – Mum, Dad, Auntie Rachel, Grandpa and Grandma.

'You all *knew*?' I said looking at their laughing faces. 'I *thought* everyone was behaving strangely. Now I know why Grandma was in the kitchen cooking all yesterday and today.'

'Talking of which,' announced Grandma, 'food's up – in the dining room.

'It's just a little snack to celebrate,' she said as we all

149

trundled inside. 'It's not often I have my whole family together in one place.'

'Little snack' was the understatement of the year.

'Are you *sure* you've prepared enough food?' said Dad as we surveyed the scene before us. The large table was groaning with food.

'Have you invited the local rugby team as well?' laughed Auntie Rachel.

'This will be a hard act to follow,' said Mum.

My eyes went straight to a huge meringue decorated with raspberries and cream. All sorts of cheeses were set out on a large colourful dish. There were dips and hummus surrounded by sticks of carrot, celery and cucumber, home-made bread, cakes, biscuits, quiches and sausage rolls – yummy! And olives – yuck!

'Yes, you've surpassed yourself this time, my love!' Grandpa said. 'It's like we're welcoming back the prodigal son. But in this case it's the prodigal grandson!' He chuckled at his own joke.

In piano lessons, I learnt about minor and major chords. Yesterday, when the farm felt lonely and deserted it was definitely a sad, minor key day. Now, with everyone around me eating, laughing and talking all at once, things suddenly felt positive and hopeful – definitely a major key day.

I picked up a glass. I filled it with juice and held it up high.

'Here's to everyone and to Willowfield Open Farm!' I shouted above the din.

'To everyone and Willowfield Open Farm!' everyone echoed back loudly!

Chapter 34

THE STREAM

'Come down to the stream!' I said to Gabriel. We'd finished eating and could barely move. 'It's still so hot. We can paddle.'

'The stream, is it?' said Grandpa who was on his way over to the tractor.

'Hop on. I'll take you there,' he said, hoisting himself up behind the wheel. 'I've got to go there and pick up those old fence posts.'

Soon we were bump, bumping down the track to our favourite place in the world. The stream marked a boundary between Willowfield and the neighbouring farm and was hidden by the tall thin trees.

Grandpa dropped us off as near as he could and we picked our way through the white flowers between the leafy canopy that let through long, delicate rays of light. This bit of woodland above the stream is known as the ash tree *bed*. The word always made me laugh. You wouldn't want to lie down there with all the prickly brambles and creepy crawlies.

'Those trees have been coppiced,' Grandpa said. He likes to explain things about the countryside. 'Coppicing has been done for centuries,' he continued. 'You cut the trees down near the ground to let the new tall, thin shoots grow. They provide wood for poles and such like. Though, I must say, I haven't cut the wood back myself for a long time – not like in the old days.'

There were plenty of old logs scattered near the stream. In the past, people put fallen trees over the rushing water to reach the other side, but now they were old and slippery. Mostly, Gabriel and I would sit on the big flat rock near the small waterfall and watch the sunlight sparkle off the water. If you shut your eyes and listen, the sound of the water falling down the rocks is like a soft, gurgling music.

As we approached, we could see someone was sitting on *our* rock in *our* stream, throwing stones into the waterfall. It could only be one person, *the* last person we wanted to see right now! It was Christopher King!

'What's he doing in our stream?' said Gabriel.

'Not your stream,' he said, without turning around. 'This stream runs between both our farms, so obviously it belongs to us too.'

He was using that know-it-all voice of his. He likes to think he knows way more than us. He might be a school year ahead of us but honestly it really doesn't show.

Gabriel put his hand out to stop me from arguing back.

'It's *ours*,' said Gabriel. 'But sit there if you want. You have our permission.'

We found a log and sat down facing the other way.

'"You have our permission",' mimicked Christopher nastily.

'Soon it won't matter anyway,' he said, turning around and grinning his sneaky evil grin.

We didn't know what he meant but Gabriel and I knew what to do – just ignore him and don't answer.

'I haven't heard anything more about your famous Open Farm,' added Christopher loudly trying to attract our attention. 'Such a shame it's not happening anymore.'

I swivelled round and glared at him. Gabriel tried to stop me.

'Well *we* haven't heard anything more about your so-called West Country Experience.'

Christopher stared straight at me with his lips pursed together.

'That's because we've got bigger plans,' he snarled, angry spittle flying from his mouth.

Neither of us wanted to play his silly game. We didn't ask what he meant. We turned our backs and put our toes into the cool water. But Christopher was obviously itching to talk.

'Yes, my dad's got big plans – way bigger than before,' he gloated, raising his voice again. 'Just you wait and see. They're all drawn up, ready to go.'

When he got no reaction, he raised his voice even higher. 'Next year there'll be polytunnels stretching all down those fields leading to the stream. And all the way up there,' he added, stretching his arm in the direction of Willowfield.

'Such a shame it means we need to buy your precious little farm. Then you'll be stuck in London.'

I looked at Gabriel. He put his fingers to his lips and shook his head but I couldn't sit still.

'That's what *you* think,' I hurled back at him. 'You don't know ANYTHING about OUR PLANS.' My words felt foolish and childish. In that moment, I hated Christopher King more than ever.

'Not interested in your pathetic plans,' said Christopher, tossing his head backwards.

Maybe Christopher didn't like it that we were two against one but suddenly he got off the rock, put his shoes on and climbed up the bank into his farm, slowly disappearing from view.

Trust him to ruin everything! I thought. We reclaimed our rock and enjoyed having the stream to ourselves. We didn't talk. It felt good to sit quietly for a while but eventually, I had to ask.

'Do you think he meant it about those polytunnels and trying again to buy the farm?'

Gabriel shrugged his shoulders. I looked at his face. He was deep in thought.

'I don't know what they're up to,' he finally said. 'All I know is we need to get our Open Farm started as soon as possible!'

Chapter 35

SO MUCH TO DO

'Hello! Hello! All I can see is your ear! Can you see me?'

I knew at once who it was. Not only the Canadian accent but the loud giggling told me it was Juliette! When I realised it was a video call, I moved the phone from my ear and looked at the screen. There she was, complete with her toothy trademark grin.

'Yes, I can see you!' I laughed. 'Where are you?'

'We're in Cornwall, silly!' She sounded surprised. 'Didn't you get my card?'

'Yes,' I said. 'It's up on the kitchen dresser for everyone to see.

'I'm sorry I haven't rung you much. So many things have happened since I last saw you,' I said.

Juliette listened wide-eyed as I filled her in on the news.

'And now Christopher King is trying to frighten us with his dad's latest scheme. He's still going on about buying up the farm.'

Juliette gasped. 'That's BAD!'

'So we're going to open the farm to the public as soon as we can, even though Moonlight hasn't recovered enough to be the star of the show – not yet anyway. Everybody's rushing around like crazy trying to get things ready.'

Juliette went quiet. Then I heard her take a deep breath and say with a rush, 'Why didn't you tell us? We want to be there for the opening. Dave and Tammy wanted to be with you guys. Me too! We all wanted to help.'

I could hear the disappointment in her voice. And see it in her face.

'It's only just been decided,' I explained. 'We're just going to skip the big official Opening Day for now.'

Juliette's reaction to that shocked me. She let out a long wail as if she was having a massive stomach ache.

'Whatever's the matter?' I asked.

'Oh, never mind!' she said.

'Well, come as soon as you can. Gabriel and I are here all summer. He wants to meet you and Dave and Tammy.'

I realised that Juliette had ended the call.

That's strange, I thought, but for now I had other things to worry about. And a lot to do. We all had a lot to do.

I hurried over to the cuddle barn to help Grandma who was settling in a brood of tiny chicks. Already there were loads of baby guinea pigs scurrying around in their large wooden pen – grey ones, sandy-coloured, black and white, deep brown, all adorable! The little chicks looked like tiny yellow pom-poms bouncing up and down.

'Hello!' Grandma said. 'I was wondering where you were.'

'Just talking to Juliette – a video call,' I said. 'Where's Gabriel?'

'In the children's play area. He's helping Grandpa paint that old tractor a nice bright blue. We need to brighten it up if the children are going to sit on it.'

'And I need to help Rachel with the display area,' I said. 'When is she coming?'

'She won't be too long,' said Grandma. 'She and your mum and dad are in the village contacting everyone about the Open Farm. They're speaking to the local newspaper and letting all the schools and nursery groups know.'

She looked at her watch.

'Well, I'm off to make some cakes. We're going to need plenty.'

When Auntie Rachel arrived, she had a folder full of signs, posters and notices. She spread them all out to decide which went where.

'The big messages about washing your hands will go on the wall in the wellington boot area,' she said, 'by the toilets and washbasins.

'And we'll put your cartoon at the entrance. I love your green googly germ! That'll get the message across!'

She went back out to the car and reappeared minutes later with a big pile of enormous boards.

'There! What do you think?' she said laying them on the table. 'I went to the Quick Print Shop with our old black and white photos from the time capsule. They've printed them out large-scale and laminated them.'

I was speechless.

'There's a whole history lesson in these photos,' said Auntie Rachel.

We studied the photos of our great-grandfather

standing by the front door of the farmhouse with the big key, the long-ago harvest scenes, and the strange-looking farm machinery.

'Wow! These look great!' said Gabriel wandering in. 'I like your cartoon as well, Abigay. Oh, and there's the really old tractor. We've just finished painting that!'

I didn't say anything. I just smiled. I was suddenly feeling warm and fuzzy. Gabriel was back on the farm where he belonged and we were about to embark on a whole new adventure! I just hoped with all my heart that everything would go to plan.

Chapter 36

FULL STEAM AHEAD

Gabriel and I were back in our old room with the bunk beds. He always used to have the top bunk but not anymore. It was MINE! At least until he could climb up easily again.

'When you are completely better, maybe I'll let you have the top bunk back,' I said, looking down to Gabriel with a grin. 'That's if I don't get too used to it up here.'

Gabriel didn't reply. I couldn't believe it. He was already asleep! I thought I'd be able to fall asleep easily too but no such luck. The events of the day were still buzzing around in my head.

Mum and Dad had been round the lanes till dark putting official brown signs on all the key signposts. They finished by erecting the big colourful sign on strong posts by the turn-off to the farm. It seemed like forever since Juliette and I helped Tammy paint it.

'That's the last task of the day,' said Mum after we had rolled the huge hay bale with the smiley face into position.

We stood back to admire our work.

'Just in time before the balloon goes up,' added Dad grinning.

I must have fallen asleep because that's when things got weird. I was suddenly standing on top of the huge round hale bale swinging an enormous flag and waving in busload after busload of people into Willowfield Farm. Next minute, I was running madly along the forest trail with Gabriel chased by giant carved animals. Except Gabriel couldn't run.

'Just go!' he yelled. 'Save yourself!'

I emerged from the trees and kept running. I was passing row upon row of polytunnels until I rounded a corner and came face to face with Christopher King sitting high on the newly painted blue tractor.

'Time to go back to London,' he screamed. 'I told you we were going to take your farm.'

In the distance I could see a convoy of cars making their way along the lane to the main road – the Three Macs, Auntie Rachel, Mum and Dad, Grandpa and Grandma – all vehicles groaning with the weight of piled-high furniture. The world faded into darkness.

By the time morning came, I was exhausted!

Still, no time for lie-ins, onwards and upwards. As Miss Davies would say, this was the first day of the rest of our lives.

It was still the same old farm but this Saturday everything was different. Soon anyone and everyone would be free to wander all over the place. And we would have to talk to people and be super-friendly – there was a flutter of butter-flies flapping around my insides.

The parking area in the top field – the Three Macs' field we now called it – soon began to fill up. Something had worked, I thought. Maybe the advert in the local newspaper.

Two families arrived that I recognised from the Village Fete. Then four cars arrived together and a crowd of children from the church Sunday school spilled out. The leader was running around frantically counting heads.

Mum collected the entrance fee money and Gabriel and I stamped people's hands with a paw print to show they had paid.

'The cats are the one animal people won't see!' I laughed. 'And Moonlight, of course.'

'Actually it's a tiger print,' said Auntie Rachel. 'They were clean out of cat paws. Let's hope nobody notices!'

Later, Gabriel and I mingled with the crowds and did our best to answer questions.

Grandma explained about feeding the different animals.

'You can throw these vegetables into the field for the pigs but do *not* hand anything to them. Pigs do bite!'

She helped the children scatter grains for the hens.

'If you feel very brave, you can let them peck from your hand!' she said.

It was such a shame that we didn't have time to build my goat mountain or get any alpacas but, on the plus side, Grandpa had managed to borrow a clean-looking trailer for the ride round the farm. Gabriel helped Grandpa keep up the running commentary, that is until the enormous Hereford bull started to wee as we passed. It weed...and weed...and weed. The children screamed with laughter. Gabriel tried not to laugh too. He studied his shoes as if he'd only just discovered them and Grandpa gazed thoughtfully off into the distance.

As the weekend continued, more locals arrived, some we knew and some we didn't but everyone was enjoying the animals, the displays and the tea shop. The sculpture trail was a huge hit.

On Monday morning another big local nursery group rattled onto the farm in two minivans. The toddlers were herded into the barn. They gazed in wonder at the roof high above and shrieked with excitement as their voices echoed around the space. Most of them had probably never been in such a big building.

They were harder to round up than the chicks but eventually we settled them down on the hay bales. Grandma started her talk.

'Little fluffy yellow chicks might look like tiny soft toys,' she explained. 'But actually they have very delicate bones.'

She showed the children how to make little nests with her hands.

'Now it's your turn,' she said as she watched everyone practise what they'd been shown. 'Remember, just like us, chicks don't like to be squashed.'

The children squealed as Grandma and I gently handed out the little yellow bundles of fluff and then suddenly everyone was huddled in hushed concentration.

When the chicks had been handed back safely, Grandma turned to the children once again.

'Before you go and see the bigger animals, come and see the baby guinea pigs in their enclosure.'

They all tiptoed forward and we spent a few moments watching the busy little creatures. When the children started squeaking and bouncing around like guinea pigs themselves, Grandma figured it was time to lead them back out into the sunshine.

It was after we waved off the overexcited nursery kids, that things began to change.

Chapter 37

GLOOM

Dad wandered around like a lost soul. He had taken charge of the children's play area, but by Monday afternoon no more children had come.

The café that was bustling all weekend, was now suddenly empty.

The rest of the day was quiet. Apart from a teenage couple who spent the whole time in the sculpture trail and an older woman who studied the old photos, nobody came. The rest of the week was the same. It was as if a tap had been turned off. We came to a terrible realisation – our big plan wasn't working.

On Friday evening, we were all sitting in the café area looking at heaps of uneaten cakes and scones. Grandma was shaking her head sadly.

'Well, it's a shame to waste these,' sighed Mum offering a plateful around.

I chose chocolate but honestly, the last thing I felt like doing was eating cake. It stuck in my throat and made me feel awkward and uncomfortable.

When Grandpa entered and saw everyone munching away, he grunted.

'I'm not hungry,' he said when Mum held out the plate to him.

He then turned around and walked away, hunched and defeated. Everything about him spoke sadness. It was more than I could bear. Grandpa's silence was even worse than his anger. I would have preferred him to just shout at us and say what he was thinking.

It was then that it really hit me. In trying to help, I'd just made things worse – ten times worse.

And it was all my fault. I'd convinced Gabriel and together we'd convinced everyone else. And all this time we thought Christopher King was wrong and we were right.

In that moment, I couldn't even bear to look at Gabriel. I couldn't bear to look at anyone. What I wanted now most in the whole world was to walk out into the field in front of the café area and have it open up and swallow me whole.

In the days that followed, I wandered around the farm like a zombie – a very guilty zombie who felt foolish and embarrassed! I was grateful to Gabriel for not rubbing it in and not blaming me for the disaster. We both felt awful but we knew well enough to let each other be, to just be there for each other. It's a twin thing.

Auntie Rachel tried to distract us.

'Let's see how Moonlight is doing,' she chirped but I knew she was just trying to make us feel better.

Grandma put an arm around my shoulders and squeezed me tight.

'Don't you worry, darling,' she said. 'You did your best and that's what counts.'

But it didn't work. I could feel she was upset too – upset and worried.

Grandpa was another story altogether. We hadn't spoken a word to each other since the day of the cakes. We did our best to avoid each other. And that wasn't the worst part. I felt I had let down the person I admired so much, even if I had never told him so.

'I'm not throwing good money after bad,' I heard him say to Grandma.

'The experiment is over! And that's final!'

But where had we gone wrong, I kept asking myself.

Gabriel's website was a true work of art. The design looked so professional and the message was bright and clear. There were some great photos of the animals – Rosie the donkey and Moonlight with his little nose and eyes peeping over the stable door. But what's the use of an amazing website if nobody visits it?

And yes, lots of people visited on the first few days but they were all locals coming to support us. They weren't likely to visit a second time. And if they did spread the word it would be to other locals.

We had advertised in the local paper but who read the local paper? Yes, you've guessed – locals!

Beyond the local area, no one knew about Willowfield Open Farm. Let's face it, we didn't have the skills or the money to spread the word properly – it was bound to fail. We were farmers, not marketing people. What did we know?

Life on the farm wasn't much fun after that. Auntie

Rachel did her best, breezing in whenever she could but it didn't make any difference.

Grandpa started to eat his meals alone in the farm office.

It didn't help either that Mum and Dad soon had to go back to work. The rest of us carried on at the farm, each under our own dark cloud, aware that we were heading towards the day when a terrible decision would have to be made – a decision that would change everything!

As the deep gloom descended on Willowfield, even the animals were getting depressed.

That is all except the pigs who continued to feast on stale scones and cakes for breakfast, dinner and tea.

Chapter 38

THE CONTRACT

Around midday, storm clouds began to gather. The air was hot and humid.

In the afternoon, Mr King drove up. Grandpa met him at the gate. They disappeared into the kitchen, shutting the door behind them.

I could NOT believe that Christopher had tagged along. There he was, as large as life, stepping out of the Range Rover. He swaggered around worshipping the family's new toy.

'It's new!' he said, stroking the bonnet. 'What do you think?'

Gabriel and I said nothing – we just glared at him.

A sudden clap of thunder made us jump. It was followed by huge drops of rain and then the real downpour began. We ran into the farmhouse and huddled around the kitchen range to dry off.

Mr King and Grandpa were already sitting at the kitchen table. Papers and files were spread out everywhere.

Auntie Rachel and Grandma came and shooed us off

to the snug at the other end of the kitchen. Christopher headed straight for the big comfy armchair. He beamed. I could hardly bear to look at him lording it over us in *our* kitchen, in *our* farmhouse. Gabriel and I sat, each in our own bubble of fear.

This was the most *dreadful* day of my life.

And to make matters even worse there was a television programme on in the background about the crisis in modern farming. That's all I needed. The presenter was droning on and on about small farmers…low yields…climate change… debt burdens. It was just unbearable but I felt too numb to get up and switch it off.

I looked over to the table where Grandpa and Mr King were sitting.

Grandpa was holding up his hand.

'Fred, don't rush me. If I'm going to sign it, I intend to take the time to read it!'

'Oh really, let's get this done Edward!' said Mr King, drumming his fingers on the table. 'It's not as if you have any choice. If you had listened to me before you would have got a better deal. But it's still the best thing you can do now.'

For a while nobody spoke, then Mr King continued.

'Once you've paid off your debts and sold all the animals, you'll have enough to afford a nice little house in the village, and a tidy lump sum to live off.'

If Grandpa looked defeated before, it was nothing compared to what he looked like now. His whole body seemed to collapse.

I watched in horror as he slowly picked up the fountain pen and held it poised, ready to sign.

This was it, the moment we had all been dreading.

Then I heard my name mentioned but it wasn't by anyone in the room. I looked towards Gabriel who was staring, mouth hanging open, pointing. I followed his gaze to the television screen.

A faintly familiar face was talking on the screen. Suddenly, it hit me. I was gobsmacked.

'That's Gina Price!'

What she was saying made me double gobsmacked!

'Grandpa,' I said. 'GRANDPA!'

Grandpa glanced over, irritated, pen hovering.

'Come QUICKLY!' I pleaded. 'They're talking about us on TV! This could change everything!'

Grandpa put the pen down.

'It's Rob's mother – the famous film-maker Gina Price. The lady we met at the art exhibition. She's talking about Willowfield!'

'Let's finish this, shall we Edward,' said Mr King.

Grandpa raised his hand once more to silence him.

The words 'Abigay's grandparents own a small Herefordshire farm' were coming from the television.

He scraped back his chair and stood tall.

'Hold on a moment!' he said. He came over and stood glaring at the television screen.

Now it was Christopher's turn to gape. He was over by the kitchen table in a flash.

'Dad!' he said, panicking.

'Someone turn the volume up!' It was Auntie Rachel who appeared from nowhere. Grandma was close behind.

Gina Price was still talking.

'Like I said, a young girl called Abigay inspired me. She initially planted the seed for this project. I've done a lot of filming abroad but what she said led me to think about what is going on here… So right now I'm planning a new documentary series on farming in this country.'

'So who exactly is this young girl Abigay?'

'I met her at the hospital where my son and her twin brother Gabriel were being cared for. She asked me if I would film her grandparents' farm. They are opening it up to the public as a way to earn extra money.'

'Hasn't that been done by others?' the interviewer interrupted. 'What's special about this?'

'I felt really moved by Abigay's story. It brought home to me the urgent need for small farms to change and adapt if they want to survive.'

The picture turned away from Gina's face to shots of trees being planted, fields of wildflowers, flooded fields, people draining the land. Then the camera turned back to Gina.

'As you know,' she continued, 'there has been a lot of talk about global warming and climate change recently. This is all going to affect how farmers produce our food. Really *big* changes are going to be needed.

'Ideally,' she carried on, 'I'd like to put Abigay's particular farm at the centre of my story. It illustrates well how the grandparents represent tradition – clearly very important – and the youngsters represent the future and the need to look forward.'

'And when does filming start?' asked the interviewer.

'I'm hoping to start filming at the farm very soon – once I've consulted with Abigay and her family.'

Mr King had moved over to where Grandpa was standing. He held out the pen to Grandpa.

'Here, Edward,' he said. 'You were about to sign this.'

Grandpa gave him a look that could have turned him to stone. He took the contract and very slowly ripped it in half. He handed it back to Mr King and looked at me. I could see the hint of a smile.

'Abigay,' he said, 'you tell him!'

I turned to Mr King, cleared my throat and said loud and clear, 'Mr King, Willowfield is not for sale! Not now! Not EVER!'

Mr King gave a weary sigh.

'I have to hand it to you, Edward. That young grandaughter of yours is a force to be reckoned with. But you'll regret this.' He hesitated, fumbling as he stuffed the torn papers into his pocket.

'Come along, Christopher.' He gathered together the rest of his of papers. 'There's nothing more for us here.'

Christopher just stood there, mouth opening and closing like a confused goldfish.

Chapter 39

NEW DAWN

I unlocked the kitchen door and stepped out into the pre-dawn chill. It was still dark. One of the farmyard cats strolled out of the shadows, looked at me puzzled, then ambled away.

I settled down on the bench in front of the kitchen window. Not long afterwards, Gabriel appeared slopping a mug of tea over the flagstones and dragging the blanket from the sofa. He sat down, draped the blanket around us both and offered me a half-eaten iced bun. I waved it away.

We sat in silence – Gabriel slurping his tea, me deep in thought.

It's amazing what being mentioned on television can do. Suddenly everyone in the village wanted to stop and chat to us. Teenagers kept asking for selfies and one little old lady even asked for our autographs.

Then, TV West picked up the story. They seemed interested in the whole grandparents/grandchildren thing and it wasn't long before we were plastered all over the local paper – '**local twins set for stardom in new Gina Price documentary**'.

And it wasn't just locally. People started to arrive at the farm from all over. Some had seen the television programme or read about us on the Country Folk site. Word got around.

'You know what really surprises me?' I said, partly to Gabriel and partly to myself. 'It's when families come from abroad. You remember that French family who came across your website and visited yesterday. It's great that you learnt those skills while you were at the hospital.'

Pictures of us were popping up all over the internet. There were pictures of Beauty, Moonlight, Rosie the donkey, the goat mountain, the chicks, the cats, the barn, the café, not to mention the sculpture trail.

The trickle of people to the farm had turned back into a stream – we even had to employ the postwoman's daughter Ruby to run the café. It wasn't long before she took full charge and started to boss the customers around like a drill sergeant. She became one of the attractions herself – people found her scary, hilarious and entertaining all at the same time.

'Who knows what else will happen when Gina's documentary finally hits our screens!' I said.

Gabriel nodded. 'It'll go stratospheric.'

For a long time we sat without talking. Apart from the noise of Gabriel slurping, I could hear an insistent blackbird in the pear tree by the kitchen door and a cow and calf mooing in the distance.

A weird howling – something between a yodel and a cat being stepped on – came from the direction of the milking shed. We looked at each other and burst out laughing.

'Grandpa's singing again,' said Gabriel.

That was a new – if not a tiny bit weird – development. Calm descended again.

Grandpa's cheeriness wasn't the only change about the place. I had changed too. I felt hopeful. Now that I had seen how change was possible, I began to think of what else we could do.

When James, the young farmer, was helping us build the goat mountain he had told us a lot about his course at the local agricultural college. They were learning about managing farms in environmentally sustainable ways, letting parts of farms go back to nature. They call it "wilding".

One wet afternoon I saw a programme on television about organic farming. Apparently, it takes a few years to achieve, but maybe that is a possibility as well…

Recently, there were so many ideas going round in my head. There was so much we could experiment with.

Of course, I hadn't mentioned any of this to anyone yet, especially Grandpa.

'Rome wasn't built in a day,' as Miss Davies would have said.

By now, the darkness had slowly lifted and given way to mauve and pink clouds floating in a glowing orange sky. We watched the changing colours. I felt ready to embrace all the good things coming our way.

I turned and looked at Gabriel.

'Gina and her crew should be arriving any time now!'

Right on cue, we saw a glint of reflected light from the newly risen sun at the entrance to the drive. Two minutes later, a heavy vehicle did a complete turn and pulled up in the yard in front of us with a loud scrunch of tyres. That was the moment the cockerel chose to crow an extra-vigorous cock-a-doodle-doo! You couldn't have planned it better.

Chapter 40

FIFTEEN MINUTES OF FAME

'Hello twins!' said Gina, beaming as she jumped down from the black transit van.

She looked very different this time. She was wearing cargo pants and a light-coloured safari vest with way too many pockets.

Even as she was shaking our hands, she was taking in everything. Her eyes darted from the farmhouse to the barn and back, then all the way down the path to the pigs in their pens.

The side door slid open and a huge man unfolded his long legs and emerged. He stretched tall and scratched his red beard with a tattoo-covered hand. He looked over at us and winked.

At the same time, a blonde woman in too-big dungarees and heavy boots jumped down from the passenger seat.

A young lad struggled out of the back where all the equipment was stacked.

'Everyone, say hello to the twins,' said Gina. 'Abigay

and Gabriel, meet Lucy – camerawoman, Jock – sound engineer, and Peter – third year film student.

'Grab these, Peter, will you?' she said handing him a clipboard and a pile of notes.

'Never let it be said that we don't make our work experience people *work*,' she added.

'Lucy, can you and Jock start unloading the van?' she said turning to the other two.

Jock managed to trip over the farmyard cat who was still prowling around the yard. He stumbled and staggered for a few steps before regaining his balance.

'Oi! Jock!' yelled Gina. 'Careful with that boom! Equipment doesn't grow on trees, you know!'

Jock looked sheepish, then glanced over at us and gave a sly wink.

Auntie Rachel was next to crunch up in her car. The farmyard was filling up fast.

'First things first,' chirped Gina after the next round of introductions. 'A cup of tea and a chat! I'm parched. Lead the way, Auntie Rachel. You lovely lot go and get some shots of the sculpture trail in the meantime,' she called over to the crew. 'Tea when you get back.'

In the kitchen, Grandma was buzzing around the stove as usual. Grandpa was standing in front of the mirror flattening his hair down with gel – that was another new development!

'Mr and Mrs Woolgar, I presume,' said Gina. 'I hope you're ready for a busy day ahead!'

Later in the barn, when Jock had set up the lights, the bright beams turned the straw bales to pure gold.

We sat down where Gina indicated. It took a moment for my eyes to get used to the glare. Lucy continued to take some final shots of the guinea pigs, the little chicks, the old farm equipment and the interior of the barn. She and Gina hardly spoke; it was like each one knew what the other was thinking – a bit like me and Gabriel.

When Gina was ready, Lucy was already in position with the camera, ready to roll.

'Now, Abigay,' Gina said with a smile, 'this is your moment. Relax, forget the camera, look towards me and tell me your story. How did it all begin?'

I felt awkward at first but then, once I started, I couldn't stop.

I told her about Moonlight being born at midnight and how it reminded me of the newborn donkey foal at the city farm. I talked about our fears and worries for Willowfield, about the plan and how it became mine and Gabriel's thing. I spoke about Grandpa and how he resisted all suggestions at first.

I talked about Grandpa's time capsule being accidentally dug up and how that moment had changed everything.

'Perfect!' said Gina when I had finally finished. 'Gabriel, what would you like to add?'

Jock moved the fuzzy boom mic in his direction.

I couldn't believe what Gabriel said. He talked about his time in hospital when he couldn't walk, how what kept him going was news from the farm.

'Making plans with Abigay gave me something to focus on,' he said.

'It gave me a goal and a reason to get better as quickly as possible. For Abigay and me, the farm means everything, you see, and the thought of losing it was something I couldn't bear thinking about.'

'And what about your own dreams for the future?' Gina asked. 'Have you thought about that?'

Gabriel answered straight away. 'I used to think I would like to be a vet, but now I want to go to the agricultural college. Then I'd like to work on the farm.'

'Good job, kids,' said Gina. 'That's a wrap. Now let's go out and mingle – keep the camera rolling, Lucy.'

When we emerged blinking from the barn, we couldn't believe what we saw.

Chapter 41

IT'S A WRAP

The place was heaving with people. It looked like the entire local population was there, not to mention hordes of strangers too. Car doors were slamming continually way off in the upper field.

'Word must have got around,' said Gina. 'You wouldn't believe how often that happens. Everyone wants to be on TV...fifteen minutes of fame and all that.'

That's when I noticed Grandpa climbing the steps to the door that leads to the observation platform over the milking parlour. He had a hammer in his hand and a mouth full of nails.

'What on earth...?' I said.

'Classic Grandpa,' laughed Gabriel as he watched him tackle a loose bit of wood hanging down across the doorway.

'The mark of a man is in the quality of his work,' Grandpa always says.

Now he was worried the visitors would judge him. Not to mention the shame of having it recorded forever on film.

He was starting to attract quite an audience too.

'Go on, Edward,' someone bellowed. 'Give us a speech!'

That got a laugh. It wasn't long before others were joining in.

'Speech! Speech! Speech!' they cried, clapping and cheering.

Grandpa looked surprised. The clapping got louder.

'Oh flip!' muttered Gabriel. 'I think he's actually going to say something. Let's hope he doesn't start singing again!'

Grandpa held his arms up. Everyone went silent. Somewhere off in the play area a small baby gave a short cry.

He looked across the crowd. I followed his gaze and saw Mr King and Christopher slipping in at the back.

Grandpa cleared his throat.

'It's a great, great pleasure to welcome so many old friends and newcomers at Willowfield today,' he said in a loud clear voice.

Gina signalled to Lucy who positioned herself to one side of Grandpa, followed by Jock who stood with the mic nearby.

'I grew up with many of you,' Grandpa continued. 'And I've watched your children grow too, as mine did. As farmers we've learnt together to handle the good times and the bad times.' He paused.

There was absolute silence.

'It was only when looking at some old photos that I realised I was part of a chain that reaches back over the years,' he said. 'Just like some of you, our family farm is part of an important tradition. And we can't let it go under! It needs to be treasured.'

Grandpa paused again.

'There was a time when I thought the chain would be broken after our elder daughter moved away to do medical research and our younger one followed her calling to be a teacher. But then along came the twins. One day I'll hand over the reins to them and it will be their turn.

'And you know, without the twins I would have lost hope – stayed stuck in the mud – and this new phase might never have begun. So friends, old and new, let's celebrate together and look forward to a brighter future!'

There was a huge burst of applause. People clapped, cheered and yelled. Someone whistled loudly. Lucy panned from Grandpa's face across the crowd. That's how she managed to film everything that happened next.

As the clapping died away, the sound of an accordion started up – it reminded me of something but I couldn't remember what.

Suddenly, at the back of the crowd a tall masked creature rose up slowly and started to advance, all the time swaying gently from side to side. People moved to let the mysterious creature pass. As it drew nearer, I could see that it was a person balanced precariously on stilts but moving confidently, swishing a beautiful cape with a big willow tree design.

The movements grew more and more frantic. The arms moved faster and faster with the music. Then the music grew quieter and the creature began to chant in a high eerie voice. 'Long Live Willowfield! Long Live Willowfield!'

With a final flourish, the mask was off and there before our eyes was a young girl, beaming and weird-looking, with warpaint and wild hair full of feathers.

'I can't believe it!' I laughed. 'Gabriel,' I said, 'meet the famous Juliette!'

The camera crew continued to circulate, filming and interviewing the locals. 'Collecting the vox pops' Gina called it.

She swooped in on Christopher King.

'So I'm guessing you're local,' she said cheerfully. 'What do you think of the Open Farm?'

Christopher went as red as a beetroot and shifted awkwardly.

'I dunno. I suppose it's alright,' he mumbled. 'If you like that sort of thing.'

He shuffled backwards and was slowly swallowed up by the crowd – end of interview. I wasn't sure if it would make the final cut.

I looked around me at busy, happy people, talking and laughing. Today was everything we could have hoped for and more, yet strangely, it all seemed unreal.

I felt like slipping away to be quiet, to be on my own – just for a bit. Gabriel wouldn't miss me. He was busy nattering away with Rob who had just arrived with his dad. Dave and Tammy were catching up with Auntie Rachel and Grandma. Juliette was still showing off her acrobatic skills to a bunch of bemused locals.

I walked over to the avenue of tall straight poplars that stand proudly on the ridge before the land slopes downhill to the stream. This will always be my best thinking place, I thought. I could hear the gentle swishing of the breeze in the leaves – one of my favourite sounds. I stood still and felt the cool air touch my face. A branch snapped and jolted me out of my thoughts. It was Grandpa.

'I suppose you wanted a bit of time to yourself, too?' he said. 'I told you we were alike, you and I.

'Is there any space there for your old grandpa?' he asked, pointing to the stile that led to the field where Moonlight and Beauty used to be – where The Accident happened so long ago.

I sat on the top bit. Grandpa sat on the step below. We listened to the sounds around us. A bee hovered near, then buzzed off again. We could hear the faint sound of evening church bells carried on the breeze.

Grandpa broke the silence.

'I got chatting to some of those young lads from the agricultural college. The college research department has obtained funding for an important farming experiment.

They have some very interesting ideas, you know.'

Grandpa waited. Was there no end of surprises with Grandpa today?

And then came the biggest surprise of all.

'They need a small farm to work with and they'd like to work with us. What do you think, Abigay?' he said.

I nearly fell off my perch. Grandpa was asking ME!

I slid down onto the step and squeezed up against my dear grandpa.

'I think you already know the answer to that,' I said.

'People will be drifting away,' said Grandpa after a bit. 'We need to get back before they send out a search party.'

We walked together back towards the farmhouse. Voices drifted across to us on the breeze.

Later that evening, we would gather all our friends and family together, friends from way back, newer friends and those who were strangers only yesterday.

We'd raise our voices and shout loudly above the roofs of the stables and barns, above the old farmhouse and the yard, the play area, the goat mountain, Ruby's Café, Rosie the donkey's shed, and Beauty and Moonlight in their field with the stars twinkling above them.

We'd shout at the top of our voices,

'Willowfield Farm Forever!'

EPILOGUE

It is autumn. Four of us are standing in the sunbeam that filters down into the barn, grandparents and grandchildren.

Now Grandpa is digging. The metal spade hits dry earth, again and again until the hole is big enough.

Grandma helps us place photos and other memories back into the old tin box, back just as it was when we discovered it forty years ahead of time.

We replace the faded photos of a man with a key and a young boy sitting proudly on an old-fashioned tractor. Then we add newer memories, a photo of Moonlight, the goat mountain and of Gabriel entertaining wide-eyed children on a trailer ride round the Open Farm.

Next to the faded newspaper cuttings we place a new crisp one about a documentary that shows a film-maker's vision of change. Lastly, we add a photo showing a red city bus with a picture of a girl along the full length of its side as she surveys the rolling green hills of Willowfield and beyond.

And then the capsule is buried, to remain hidden for another hundred years.

ACKNOWLEDGEMENTS

I am greatly indebted to many people. To Janet and David Legge, warm-hearted and delightful hosts who ran their farm Shortwood in Herefordshire as an Open Farm for twenty-five years. This was the inspiration for the story.

I learned a lot from the City Literary Institute's Children's Writing Workshop led by Penny Joelson. I am also grateful to members of Islington Writers for Children for their careful and constructive feedback, especially to Sunita and Stephanie and above all to John O'Leary.

John O'Leary deserves a special mention. He helped me over a long editing period, improved certain moments in the plot and believed in the story from the beginning. Thank you John!

The publishers SilverWood Books have been helpful at every stage and I am so glad that a writing colleague recommended them to me.

I am grateful to Patrice Aggs for her lively drawings. She captured the characters just as I saw them in my mind's eye. She illustrated my book *My Big Brother JJ* and I knew I would love her to illustrate *Abigay's Farm* if she had the time.

Thanks go to my family – to Rachel for her critical advice and for encouraging me to go ahead and get the story published. To Jo and Roger who have always been enthusiastic and to Ben who is keen to help publicise it. Lastly, special thanks to my husband Donald who has had to hear me talking about the book for some years and has been supportive and helpful throughout the long process.

ODETTE ELLIOTT has been writing stories ever since she was ten years old. When her youngest child started school, her grandmother asked, "So when are you going to send off all your stories and write some more?" This was the push that she needed.

Odette's dream came true when her picture book, *Under Sammy's Bed,* was published, followed by *Sammy Goes Flying.* Both books appeared on the BBC's TV programme *Playbus* and have been shown around the world. Two other 'Sammy' books followed. *Sammy's Christmas Workshop,* published in 1992 is still being borrowed in libraries. *My Big Brother JJ* was published in 2009 was used in SATS tests in 2019.

The 'Sammy' books are based on the fantasies of Odette's youngest child, who always pretended that he could keep up with his older brother and sisters. *Abigay's Farm* was inspired by cousins who ran an Open Farm.

Odette enjoys writing, reading, travelling – especially in the Scottish Highlands – walking in the countryside, gardening and being a grandmother.

For more information, see Odette's website and blog
http://www.odetteelliott.co.uk
Twitter @keepwritingOdet
Facebook odette elliott.5

Lightning Source UK Ltd.
Milton Keynes UK
UKHW040201151021
392206UK00001B/32